One Little
KISS

A SMART CUPID
ROMANTIC COMEDY

One Little KISS

A SMART CUPID ROMANTIC COMEDY

MAGGIE KELLEY

Entangled Publishing, LLC
2614 South Timberline Road
Suite 109
Fort Collins, CO 80525
Visit our website at www.entangledpublishing.com.

Lovestruck is an imprint of Entangled Publishing, LLC.

Edited by Vanessa Mitchell
Cover design by Erin Dameron-Hill
Cover art from iStock

Manufactured in the United States of America

First Edition May 2017

For my friends in NEORWA
Thank you for your support.
And, um, for the record...I love Ohio.

"The path to paradise begins in hell."
Dante Alighieri

The Daily Blog: Smart Cupid.com.
Posted by Senior Love Blogger, Kate Bell.

Cupids, if you (like me) wake up one morning to find your live-in boyfriend has emptied his side of the closet and left behind nothing but a box of Krispy Kremes on the Formica counter—here's what you do:

First, accept that your relationship is officially over.

Second, go get your iPod. Put Coldplay's "Fix You" (preferably the acoustic version) on repeat until you literally cannot stand to hear it anymore.

Eat three, maybe four, chocolate, cream-filled doughnuts and resist your sudden, desperate desire to re-read Dr. Phil's *Love Smart.*

It isn't healthy.

Then take a deep, seven-second breath, and on the exhale, acknowledge the fact that your track record with love is inexplicably terrible. Don't ask, "Why didn't I see this coming?"

Promise to change.

Swear (pinky swear is fine) that you will stop looking for love in all the wrong places, and never—*ever*—under any circumstances, no matter how charming he seems, no matter how often he says he needs you, date another super-hot, super-vain, pathologically shallow guy who's more interested in a quickie in the hallway than calling you the next day. That man is not The One.

No matter how hot he is.

Especially if he's hot.

Chapter One

Kate Bell, suddenly single and regretting the four doughnuts she'd eaten this morning while watching Dr. Phil On Demand, sat across from her boss and considered the idea that she might have a knack for the wrong guy.

"So, the latest Prince Charming decided to hit the road?" Jane Wright tucked the dark curls of her pixie cut behind both ears and flashed a high-wattage, suspiciously Zen smile.

Clearly the shit is about to hit the fan. The Manhattan matchmaker might look all cool and breezy, but nothing got in between her and the success of SmartCupid.com. Certainly not a friend's rant-filled, anti-dating breakup tirade.

Kate bit her bottom lip. "I guess you read my blog."

Jane pushed aside the remains of a pastrami sandwich and nodded at the glowing tablet on her desk. "Oh, I read it all right, and if the whole thing wasn't so sad, I'd tell you it was funny."

Kate winced, knowing she was in serious trouble. Not only could she lose her job, but her meltdown had undermined all the work she'd done to catch the attention of a junior editor at *Cosmopolitan*. She'd been dreaming about landing a job as the magazine's authority on Happily Ever After forever. Now she was one Google search away from working at *The Farmer's Almanac*. "Probably not such a smart move—writing an anti-love piece for a matchmaking site."

Jane snapped the tablet cover shut in one quick motion. "Probably not."

Cringing at the less-than-subtle sarcasm, an apology raced out of her faster than the D-line into the city. "I know. I'm *sorry*. I was a total train wreck this morning, especially after the closet purge, and yes, I went too far with the whole pathological man comment, but…"

"You think so?" Despite her obvious annoyance, a sympathetic frown worked its way across her friend's face. "Did he really leave a half-eaten box of doughnuts on the counter?"

"He really did."

The frown deepened. "Did he leave a rent check? A parting gift, maybe?"

Kate considered the undershirt she'd stuffed in her tote bag this morning so the apartment wouldn't reek of Irish Spring. "Not unless you count the T-shirt he left next to the doughnuts."

"I don't," she said, her eyes narrowing over the half-empty coffee cup on her desk. "Did he steal your MasterCard again?"

She shifted in her seat, hoping to avoid a rehash of the whole credit card disaster. "Not funny, Jane."

"Who was being funny?" she asked, glancing around the office. "It's a serious question."

A wave of heat infused her cheeks. "Borrowing your girlfriend's credit card *one time* does not make you a felon."

"It does if you disappear to Vegas with it, run up the bill, and refuse to pay."

"It's not like he killed somebody."

Jane tore at the edges of her sandwich wrapper. "No, he's too dumb for that."

Kate drew in a long breath. A small—thankfully, very small—part of her wanted to defend him, but her friend was right. The man had cleared out without so much as a backward glance and stuck her with the remainder of the lease. Not *technically* a felony, but *definitely* romantically criminal.

She slumped down in her chair. "I make terrible choices when it comes to men."

Silence filled the space between them, punctuated only by the sound of her boss tearing at the wrapper. "Well...not *terrible* terrible."

"No—more like *disastrously* terrible. The only question is why—*why?*" she asked the bronze Cupid perched on the edge of the desk. "I practice self-actualization, cultivate personal growth, embrace my ch'i, but hey, show me a guy with a sketchy romantic past and a working penis, and Hallelujah, I'm in love."

Jane's smile aimed for reassurance, but landed closer to sweetie-you-need-a-new-game-plan. "You've got a super-sized heart, that's all, and you're lovely and trusting and … What is the term all your self-help books use...other-oriented? You're other-oriented."

"Well, being *other-oriented* sucks." Kate yanked a loose thread from the hem of her skirt and hoped the fabric wouldn't unravel like her love life. "My super-sized heart is tired of being crushed. I'm a dating disaster. Why can't I just find The One and be done with it?"

"With dating or with love?"

"Both." A soft breath hitched at the back of her throat, and the longing in her voice broke her misguided heart all over again. "Dating *and* love."

Jane leaned forward in the upholstered chair and steepled

her fingers. "Maybe you need to try a different tactic. A change of *perspective*. What if you stopped focusing on finding The One," she said, tossing out a set of air quotes, "and started exploring more...*possibilities*?"

She looked up from her hem. "What possibilities?"

Jane let go a sigh. "A different kind of romance, one with less pressure and more potential for..."

Her mouth twisted to one side as she wondered if her love-centric heart could handle a different kind of romance. "Spontaneity?"

"That's the word. You don't have to plan everything." Jane winked. "You don't have to *plan* at all."

Don't plan? No. Just no. How did you go out with someone and not try to figure out if you had any long-term potential? Love? Marriage? Family? And Jane wanted her to just forget everything and let it be. Let it *be*?

"That doesn't sound like romance at all."

A shrug of Jane's shoulder. "I'm just saying. You can't plan passion. You want a guy who looks at you like he can't get enough of you."

Kate wrinkled her nose. Of course, she wanted a guy who looked at her like she was the be-all, end-all; she simply preferred a consciously committed relationship to spur-of-the-moment, no-strings passion. Then again, her relationship history was nothing to write home about. Not unless she wanted to give her mother another reason to marry her off to the neighbor's desperately single son back in Arcadia. *Which I do not.*

"Well...maybe," she said, negotiating with her conscience. "*Sex on the side* does sound a lot better than *dumped without a backward glance*."

"Wait—*what*?" Jane blinked several times in succession. "Did I *say* sex on the side?" She shook her head. "No, no, no. I didn't mean *sex* on the *side*. I meant something more along the lines of a new kind of relationship. One that doesn't try to plan ten steps in advance."

Kate sat up in her chair and tapped her heels against the hardwood. Not her usual modus operandi, but…

"A sweet, *non*-pathological guy might be just what I need to jumpstart the new Kate."

Her boss's brows raised in a question, probably wondering what happened to her friend, the relationship junkie. "The new Kate?"

"The *brand new* Kate." After all, her closet was half empty, she'd listened to more than enough Coldplay to last a lifetime, and change was critical.

"Brand new isn't necessarily…" Jane's phone vibrated against the vintage desk. "Damn." She eyed the number, pressed mute, and tapped the screen with her finger. "Okay. So the first step to getting you past this is…" Her phone vibrated again. "Double damn."

"What's wrong?"

"Let's just say you're not the only one who can't get a guy to do what she wants."

"Your fiancé?"

Jane cringed. "Please never mention that word in the same sentence as this person again. No, it's not Charlie; it's this situation with…" She waved away the thought. "It's my own fault for trying to get him to do the interview." She glared at her phone. "If he'd just say yes, it would be over."

Oh my.

Can you say opportunity?

She'd just wrecked her career. She wasn't about to ignore a chance to prove she was still worth her salt.

"Sounds like you could use some help," Kate said.

"Oh no. You don't want this one."

Kate put on her most confident smile and hoped it looked better than she felt. "Try me."

Jane read a text message, then sighed and put the phone down. "It's next month's interview for The Bachelor Profile."

Kate's heart leaped forward like an eight-cylinder on the open road. *The Bachelor Profile?* Talk about a dream opportunity. If she could nail that, her career wouldn't just be back on track, it would be headed into the stratosphere.

"I'm the best at convincing people to do things they don't want to do," she said.

Unless that means being with me...

"Yeah," Jane said, "you are. But this bachelor is... different. He's high-profile..."

"I can handle high-profile."

"Which means an exclusive, potentially challenging interview..."

"Challenging is great," she chimed in.

"...with a semi-retired, *totally* reclusive, *extremely* stubborn relationship expert." — Jane wrinkled her nose at the phone — "who just happens to be my brother."

And there it was — the *catch*. Kate shook her head. "But Nick isn't a bachelor or reclusive or a relationship expert."

Jane gave a short nod. "And thank God," she said. "Only room enough for one sex and relationship therapist in the family. No, I'm talking about my other brother — Jake."

"Jake? Jake *Wright*?" Kate blinked several times, her pulse suddenly zooming past its target rate. "*The* Jake Wright, bestselling author of *The Sex Factor*?"

An eye roll was all her friend could muster. "That's the one."

"*Jake Wright* is your brother?"

"Oh my God." Jane scribbled a sarcastic "yes" into the air. "*Yes.*"

This was incredible. Before he'd dropped out of sight, Jake Wright had been on everyone's hot list. His treatise on modern relationships was considered a revolutionary discussion of erotic intelligence and contemporary intimacy. And now, he was her bachelor.

If she could convince him to do the interview.

"Let me take care of this." She pulled out her phone and typed: buy copy of *The Sex Factor*. "Look at it this way: it'll make up for my meltdown this morning."

"Kate…you know I believe in you. But this would be a serious step up from the daily blogs." She inched to the edge of her Queen Anne chair. "Are you sure you're ready for this?"

Ready? Tired of being pigeonholed as the blonde from Ohio State, Kate had been dying to prove her capabilities, and if this profile helped her land the dream job at *Cosmo*, she'd have a legitimate reason to stay in New York. A glossy national magazine equaled a career in her parents' eyes, as opposed to "some job at an internet site." *Cosmo* would compel her family to take her seriously and allow her to gently turn down her dad's offer to run the family construction business back in Ohio. *Heck, yeah, I'm ready.*

This was a chance of a lifetime. "I am more than ready."

Jane leaned forward, looking every bit the Manhattan hotshot she was. "He'll be a tough sell. I've been trying for three years to get him to agree to this profile."

"*Three years?*"

"Three *years*," Jane said with a frustrated sigh. "But now he's slated as our July bachelor, so it's a done deal. Whatever he says, whatever he *does*, just roll with it."

A frown pulled at her brow. *Whatever he does?* Was he some kind of self-help guru turned axe murderer? Had he burned down a few retail stores? Skipped the country under an assumed name? C'mon, this was *Jake Wright*. The man sported a PhD and a bestseller on his résumé. *How bad can he be?*

Jane cocked a dark eyebrow in reply, as if the question

had been spoken aloud. "He won't like the idea, not one teeny tiny iota, but if you make this profile happen despite his resistance, I'll forget about the blog—maybe even call in a favor and talk to a friend who works for *Cosmo*."

There it was. The future that minutes ago she'd thought was lost. If she wanted a shot at her dream job, she needed to nail the interview as penance for this morning's ill-conceived blog. Chances were good Jane would make the call anyway, but Kate wanted to prove she deserved her friend's confidence. *This is my chance. My chance of a lifetime…*

"I'm in."

The hint of a smile touched her friend's lips, the kind that almost always meant trouble. "I'll let Jake know it's taken care of."

Too late to back out now.

• • •

"Jane, there's no way in hell I'm going to be your Bachelor of the Month."

Jake Wright forced a piece of plywood into the window frame with his shoulder and shoved a hammer into his back pocket, then clicked up the volume on his cell phone with his free hand. "No. Way. In. Hell. I've got enough on my plate right now, preparing for a little visitor known as Hurricane Dante. I'm not interested in your matchmaking."

"I'm proposing an interview, not a date, for crying out loud." His sister's exasperation filtered through the line from eleven hundred miles away. "And why are you preparing for a hurricane? What hurricane?"

"Jesus, don't you watch the news?" *If only there were a 24-hour Matchmaking Channel.*

"Are you talking about C-SPAN?" she asked. "Because… no, not if I can help it."

"I'm *talking* about basic… Listen, forget it. I'm working against the clock here, preparing for a Category 1, so sorry, but no time to entertain your love reporter."

A pause filled the line, followed by an anxious sigh. "A Category 1 is on the low end of the scale, right? Not seriously *dangerous*. Because…um…the story's kind of already slated."

"Then change it." He grabbed another plywood board. He was on the island to find peace after his ugly divorce. The last thing he wanted was a bunch of single women tracking him down for love advice. Or worse—an actual date. "Being splashed across the Internet like man candy isn't exactly a priority right now. Get back to me next month."

Not that he'd agree to be a bachelor on his sister's matchmaking site next month, either, but maybe suggesting a delay would buy him thirty days of peace.

"Next *month*?" Jane said. "No, no, no, can't be next month. You're Mr. July."

"*Mr. July?*" He set the plywood into the upper window frame. Jesus, next thing he knew he'd be sporting a pair of boxer briefs in the Smart Cupid Christmas calendar. "Forget it, Janey."

"But being interviewed as a bachelor for Smart Cupid is a once in a lifetime opportunity, like making the *Maxim* Hot List, only hotter and sexier—and male."

"I'm sure it's the chance of a lifetime for a guy who's interested in falling in love, but as we've discussed, I'm not interested in love. *Period*." He pressed his thumb and index fingers against the bridge of his nose. Exhausted by the effort to prepare the island for the storm, the last thing he needed was his sister sending a reporter he'd have to look after.

"Jake, you're a sex and relationship therapist."

"Ex–sex and relationship therapist."

"How can you not be interested in love?"

"Easy." He banged the wood into the frame. Some people

were bad bets when it came to love. Too closed off or just plain unwilling to take the risk. He wasn't necessarily proud of the fact, but he fell somewhere on that spectrum. His marriage had taught him that much.

Emotionally unavailable.

That's what women called him these days. The truth hurt, but it didn't matter how much he wanted love if he didn't feel it anymore. If he ever had at all.

"Relationships aren't for everyone."

Jane's voice cut through the wire, straight to the heart of the matter. "A life without love sounds kind of lonely to me."

Always the matchmaker.

"Yeah, well, I'm not lonely. I've got *Island Time.*" He picked up a power drill and walked across the dusty plank floor to the 1966 Chris Craft cruiser he planned to restore, his own, less official kind of therapy.

"Jake, you left Manhattan for a vacation—*three* years ago. Three years of no New York. No smog-filled air. No *Sal's Pizza.* No Mets games."

He reset the drill bit and anchored the boat to the table. "You know I'm a Yankees guy."

Truth was the city didn't define him. If he went back, it'd only be to fulfill his contractual obligations now that he was under the gun. His ex-agent had started sniffing around recently, pressuring him to deliver another bestseller, but writing a book about love relationships for the asshole who'd slept with his wife—currently ex-wife—and then *married* her? Yeah, *Island Time* and a lengthy legal battle seemed preferable.

"Don't you think it's time to come home?" she asked.

Jake rechecked the anchors and ignored the sympathy in her voice. Sure, he missed the city, but not enough to go back to that counterfeit, celebrity-style life. At the height of his career, everybody had wanted a piece of him, *especially* women. They'd line up for an autograph or marital advice, all with the hope of landing a nationally famous relationship expert. But he'd only wanted one woman. A bitter sound formed in the back of his throat. But that was a long time ago. A helluva long time. *Lesson learned.* "Jane, I have to go."

His sister let go an enormous sigh. "Okay, fine—go. But like it or not, you're Smart Cupid's Mr. July, so don't try to weasel out of it. Kate is already on the way."

He tightened his grip on the phone. "Who the hell is Kate?

"My best blogger, Kate Bell. And be nice to her. She's not exactly a frequent flier."

His jaw flexed to keep him from saying something he might regret. "Then why is she flying into a hurricane?"

"Obviously I didn't know about the storm. I'm marrying Charlie, not Jim Cantore."

Jake groaned aloud. Since her engagement, his sister mentioned her upcoming nuptials every chance she got. Every email, every phone call. *Everything* reminded *her* to remind *him*—a walk through Central Park, pizza in the old neighborhood, hell, the color *white*. At least the hurricane-as-a-reminder made sense. God knew marriage topped his list of natural disasters. "Where am I supposed to put Ms. Infrequent Flyer? The resort is fully booked."

"I don't know… Your bungalow is nice."

"My *bungalow*?" His neck began to sweat. He'd bought the island and started his couples retreat to find some damned quiet. Now he was supposed to let some Manhattan-style, sure-to-be-demanding woman named Kate into his freaking peace-filled bungalow. Not going to happen. Jake Wright was a matchmaking-free zone.

"Jake? Are you there? You're, um, breaking up." A wrapper of some kind crinkled in his ear as if it were static. "Must be the storm. I'm losing your signal."

Losing the signal, my ass.

"Jane, I mean it this time," he said through gritted teeth.

"If you can hear me, Kate arrives in Paradise Cay on the two o'clock charter."

He set the drill down carefully and dragged both hands through his hair. "Not funny."

"Sorry, bro, too much static." More wrapper crinkling.

He tried to hold onto his rapidly unraveling temper. "Jane, I refuse to be a bachelor for your website. I told you. I'm through with all that—"

"Her name is Kate. Arriving on the two o'clock. Trust me, you'll love her."

Striding toward the door on the off-chance he was wrong about the wrapper, he smashed his knee into the cabinets lining the wall and bit back an expletive. "Jane? *Jane?*"

Click.

"Dammit." He whirled back around and slammed his fist down on top of a nearby sawhorse. A hammer and a few nails fell and clattered onto the floor. The charter would land soon, provided the plane hadn't been rerouted. *Of all the times to send a love blogger to the island.* He'd spent half the night, not to mention the entire morning, preparing the island resort for Dante, and now, thanks to his matchmaking sister, he needed to hustle over to the damn airfield.

He slapped the sawdust from his paint-splattered pants and imagined this Kate Bell standing on the tarmac in the wind, rain beating against her sure-to-be tailored clothes and overstuffed luggage, New York attitude on full display.

Guilt instantly flooded his body. Attitude or no attitude, he'd never abandon anyone. Jake was not his father, a man who had walked out on his family on Christmas Eve and never looked back. He'd cop to being emotionally distant, but he was a man who stuck—and his sister knew it.

Dammit.

He shoved the prescription safety glasses hard against the bridge of his nose and grabbed his keys from the tool chest. He loved Jane. He wanted to support her, and he was proud of the way she built her company, but interviewing to be some bachelor? No.

He strode across the property toward the truck, a plan already forming in his mind. When he got to the airfield, he'd explain the situation in a calm, professional manner. Kate Bell would realize he had nothing to offer to the readership of the Cupid blog and cancel the interview on the spot. Because the truth was Jake Wright was no expert on love.

Not anymore.

Chapter Two

Maybe it's the martinis, Kate thought, shoehorned into the second row of the chartered flight direct from hell. *Please, God, let it be the martinis.*

She yanked her seat belt as the plane dipped into another air pocket. *Be calm, be calm, be calm.* They were not about to fall out of the sky. No. Her imagination was just working overtime—courtesy of the vodka. When the pilot said "final descent," he didn't mean *final* descent. He meant final for now, not final *forever.* Not *prepare-to-meet-your-Maker final. Prepare-to-meet-your-Maker final* was *not* an in-flight announcement. *Definitely the martinis.*

Besides, why worry? A bolt of lightning crackled through the clouds. Lightning was going to strike them down first. She clawed at the edges of the seat cushion/flotation device like a cast member of *Lost,* one of the few, one of the damned. Terrified, barely breathing. The landing gear screeched into position, an earsplitting metal-on-metal sound.

Holy Mother of God. A prayer formed on her lips. Her eyes slammed shut, her every muscle braced for impact, certain any second the plane would crash onto the island. *Don't panic.* She held on tight. *Do. Not. Panic.* Rubber wheels hit the dirt—once, twice, three times—the Cessna skidding furiously along the narrow runway until the engine cut back with a deafening whirr and the plane roared to a complete stop.

Jesus, Mary, and Joseph. Her shaking hand let go of the cushion, and her eyes fluttered open, tears leaking from their edges. She could breathe. Her body was trembling, but she could breathe.

She. Could. *Breathe.*

She pressed her forehead against the cool rectangular window and glanced down at the island's sweet, solid, kissable ground. *Hallelujah. Amen.*

And that's when she saw him.

Shit.

He stood alone at the edge of the runway, wearing a pair of oversized black plastic glasses, paint-splattered chinos, and an irritated expression. She took a second look. *That's my bachelor? The nationally famous sex expert? The guy in the Magoo glasses?*

She backed off the window and rifled through her paperwork for a recent publicity photograph, but she came up empty. Her brain flipped through its Rolodex of images. Author photo on the flap jacket of his book? Check. Television interview when his book had hit the top of the bestsellers list? Yep. Dark hair, blue eyes, perfect smile. That Jake Wright had been crush-worthy, a *Cosmo* girl's dream come true.

So who was this guy? His *caddy*?

Anxiety pooled in her stomach. *Just take a breather. Be kind. Be reasonable.*

No need to FREAK out. Think about it. He was her boss's brother. Her *friend's* brother. If there was a time to be open-minded, that time was now. Not all bachelors needed to be hot, right? Hell, she'd given up hotties this morning like they were chocolate and it was Lent. Of course, hers was a personal dating choice made under extreme emotional duress. Smart Cupid's readers didn't want an average-looking, non-pathological man; they wanted a smokin' hot Mr. July.

A dizzy sensation washed over her—from the stress or the martinis, she wasn't sure. *Don't hyperventilate.* She grabbed the airsickness bag from the seat pocket and snapped it open. *Breathe into the bag,* she thought, drawing in one of those seven-second breaths she'd learned at last week's "Breathe Your Way to Success" seminar. *Do. Not. Hyper*—who was she kidding? She took another peek out the window, stifled a sob, and shoved her head deeper into the bag.

"Make this profile happen despite his resistance, and I'll forget about the blog—maybe even call in a favor and talk to a friend who works for Cosmo.*"*

Her boss's words echoed through her mind. She wanted to prove her worth—to Jane, to her family, to *herself.* She needed this interview. Blow this chance and she could kiss her future good-bye.

Not an option.

She crumpled up the bag and shoved it back into the seat pocket.

Focus on Cosmo. She unbuckled the seatbelt, grabbed her tote, and wove her way toward the exit. Cosmo *byline.* She stepped onto the foldy metal stairs that led to the ivory sand. Cosmo *feature editor.* The salty, humid air clung to her skin, and she pulled at her blouse. Ignoring the looming doozy of a headache—thank you, martini number three—she visualized that byline on the pages of the magazine, the January issue, the one with the Bedside Astrologer.

"*Cosmopolitan,*" she said on an exhale, aiming for confidence.

But as her left foot hit the top stair, her kitten heel caught on the metal grid and pitched her body forward. She reached for the railing with both hands but slipped down a few steps, wincing at the ominous ripping sound that announced the torn seam at her side.

Shit, shit, shit.

She scrambled to her feet and tugged at the ripped skirt for an extra inch of coverage as her itinerary, the contracts — everything she had on her relationship expert — tumbled out of her upended tote. *No, no. no. Why didn't I bring a zippered carry-on?*

Magoo sprinted toward the plane. "Jesus, are you okay?"

"Fine." Kate anchored the useless bag onto her shoulder and smoothed her skirt over her hip, knowing there'd be a monster bruise there later. "Totally fine." Humiliated. Tipsy. A few missing documents away from losing her job. She flashed a reassuring smile, spun unsteadily around the silver staircase, and chased the papers circling beneath the plane.

He reached for her elbow, but she swiveled past him. "Miss Bell, it's not safe to go back there."

She waved him off and ducked beneath one of the wings as a gust of wind pressed her forward. "Give me one minute."

"Miss Bell, I can't do that," he said, following her under the plane.

Making little circles in the air with her index finger, she glanced back at him. "Just turn the other way. Pretend you don't see me."

A few feet away, the manila folder lay upturned on the tarmac. In an aggressive move antithetical to her "Breathe Your Way to Success" mantra, her bare foot slammed onto the edge of the folder. But unable to maintain her balance on her remaining heel, she swiveled out of control and careened toward him. Her hands caught the collar of his shirt, pulled him toward her, and — *wow.* The air rushed from her lungs. Up close, he was cute, not the gorgeous-beyond-redemption

type from his photo, but definitely more *Alias*-style Bradley
Cooper than 1940s cartoon character. Raggedy dark hair that
hit his collar, a half-cocked smile, a way-past-five o' clock
shadow.

His hands at her hips steadied her. "You okay?"

She blinked up at him, and the rush of her panic
evaporated as a sense of kismet—calm, drunken kismet—
washed over her. "Yes, yes, I'm…I'm fine. Just fine."

Her brain reached for something more, something
professional, but the way his ocean-blue eyes twinkled behind
the oversized glasses threw her tipsy thoughts for a loop. A
sudden image of his callused hands tracing the line of her
hip crashed through her martini-infused consciousness. She
released her grip and stepped back.

Whoa—no.

Her now semi-functional brain ticked off all the reasons to
take a second step back. *Boss's brother.* Smart Cupid *bachelor.*
Ticket to Cosmo. Real Kate needed to remain professional,
but New Kate wanted a side of no strings attached. *Or maybe
that's just the vodka talking.*

Definitely.

The.

Vodka.

A blush burned across her cheeks. "I'm not exactly a
frequent flyer, so I *might* have indulged in a couple of martinis."
She held up three fingers. "Two. Maybe three. Tough to know
for sure, because those promotional bottles are so cute and
tiny and…" But before she finished, his steel-toe boots were
halfway across the runway, his faded denim shirt flapping
behind him in the wind. She blinked at his disappearing form.
"Hey, where are you going?"

He pointed toward a yellow building fifty yards beyond
the runway. *Aviation Services.* "To book your flight."

"My flight?" She swung back around the foldy steps and

rushed up to yank her heel from the grid. "What about the interview?"

"Interview's off."

"Off?" Shoving the shoe back onto her foot, she stumbled after him. She'd expected some resistance, but she'd just touched down. "It can't be *off*."

He spared a backward glance. "Sorry, sweetheart, but the hurricane takes priority."

"Don't-don't call me sweetheart, *sweetheart*. I'm more than just…" Sure, she was tipsy, but that didn't give him the right to give her the sweetheart treatment, judging her blonde hair and curves. *Wait a sec…* "A hurricane? What hurricane?"

He jerked his unshaven chin toward the horizon. "The one that's headed toward the island."

"That storm"—she glanced back at the shoreline—"is an actual *hurricane* and you think I'm going to climb onto another tin can and fly out of here? *Voluntarily?*" she said, double-timing her stride to keep up. "There aren't enough martinis at an upper west side cocktail party."

A muscle ticked in his jaw, clearly irritated, but something flashed in his eyes, barely hidden. Something that felt fiercely protective. "If it wasn't safe to fly out, they'd cancel all the flights. Better you get off the island before there's any serious wind or snapped power lines."

Serious wind? Snapped power lines? "I am not flying."

He shaded his eyes and looked through the window. "The resort's booked."

A familiar panic started in her chest. *Oh God, don't hyperventilate. Do. Not. Hyperventilate.* "There must be one available room on this godforsaken—"

"No rooms. Completely booked."

"I could stay with you," she said, emboldened by the powerful combination of desperation and martinis. "Get the up close and personal."

"Stay?" His body angled toward her, annoyance carved into his face. "With me?"

"It's one night." She focused in on him. He was still irritated. Made it hard to appeal to his gentler side. "Jake — can I call you Jake? — Jake, this interview is...well, it's a major opportunity for me, and if you don't give me a break and answer a few easy questions — long story, short — I could end up in Ohio." She fought back the rising panic, seven seconds from going to pieces. "Have you ever *been* to Ohio?"

"Ohio? What the hell is wrong with —" His annoyance again was replaced by a flash of...yep, definitely concern. So he did have a weak spot, confirmed when he held up both palms in a gesture of surrender. "You know what? I don't need to know. You can stay."

"Really?" *Thank you, thank you, thank you.* Not as tough a sell as expected. If it weren't for the irritation and bad attitude, she'd plant a big one on him right now. "I promise you won't regret this interview."

"You can stay the night." He rubbed the grime from the window and tapped on the glass. A sign hung over the desk. ALL FLIGHTS CANCELED. "But as for the interview? No way in hell."

Her grateful spinning world skidded to a stop. *Wait a sec. No way in hell?* Had he missed the part about the looming possibility of O-hi-o? "You can't just cancel the interview."

"I can." He gestured down the runway at the clouds gathering in the sky. "But if you'd prefer to spend the night here in Aviation Services... It's not the most secure building on this *godforsaken* island, but..."

"You wouldn't." She raised her chin in a challenge.

He jammed the Elvis Costellos into the bridge of his nose. "Try me."

Gazing up at him, Kate gauged the likelihood that he'd leave her stranded. Probably too responsible, considering the glasses and the chinos, but with three martinis coursing through her veins, her judgment *might* be impaired. "Fine."

Jake gave a short nod. Pressed his lips into a firm line. And strode off toward the Cessna. Halfway there, he stopped to talk to the ground crew and tipped his head toward the hangar, offering what looked like directions before continuing toward the plane.

She lurched away from the door, vodka messing with her equilibrium, the screen banging behind her as she raced to catch him. "If I could just ask a couple of questions—off the record."

"What part of *no interview* do you not understand?" He yanked her duffle with its neon pink Smart Cupid tags from the underside of the plane, slung it across his shoulder, and stalked over to a truck parked at the edge of the airfield.

Kate stopped, a small voice inside her whispering, *Give the guy a break. He's not interested in being the bachelor. Just forget the interview and hunker down with some Ho Hos, a couple magazines, and a bottle of Chardonnay.* But a second voice, a louder, drunken voice said, *Let this sucker off the hook and you're going home with no interview and no shot at* Cosmo. *A blonde, brokenhearted failure.*

The drunken voice won.

She rushed forward on her damaged heel. "Being a hunk for Smart Cupid is a once in—"

"A lifetime opportunity." He tossed the bag into the bed of the pickup and secured it under the tarp. "I've heard the company line, Miss Bell."

"So why not grab the brass balls? Or, ring. I mean—grab the brass ring." *Damn, that didn't sound right.* She pressed a palm to her forehead and tried to organize her thoughts.

He yanked at the overlong curls at the back of his neck. "Despite what your boss may have told you, I'm not interested in love."

Hold everything. Not interested in love? He was the expert. Her heart kicked in its reflexive response. "*Everyone's* interested in love."

"Not everyone." The truck's tailgate slammed into place. "Definitely not me."

Kate stared back at him, her thoughts all jumbled together from the martinis…and the flying…and the hurricane. "Look, don't take this the wrong way, but maybe love's not the problem. I mean, I know you're the authority on the subject…"

"Ex-authority on the subject." He fished his keys from the pocket of his chinos and let the beep of his auto-starter punctuate his words.

"…but maybe you've been looking in all the wrong places."

He cocked a dark eyebrow. "There are right places?"

Like she needed his sarcasm right now. Where were all the good guys? The romantic ones who climbed fire escapes, flowers at the ready. "You just haven't found The One."

"Right. The One." That muscle in his jaw ticked again, all cynical and derisive. "Sounds like three martinis talking." He opened the passenger door and waved her inside.

"No, no, no, definitely not the martinis talking," Kate said, depositing her butt inside the front cab. "Okay, maybe they're talking *a little*. But they're talking sense." He moved to shut the door, and she stopped it with her kitten heel. "Can I tell you something?"

"Can I stop you?"

She scooted to the edge of the leather seat. "Here's the deal. I suck at dating."

His head fell forward on a sigh. "Please get in the truck."

Balancing her hands on his shoulders, she continued, "Seriously. I do. All kinds of dating. My one and only blind date actually had a warrant out for his arrest. Halfway through dinner, the police dragged him from our table in the back of this little Thai place in Queens. I spent the rest of the night scouring line-ups downtown."

His eyes snapped to hers. "Jesus—really?"

Kate nodded. "Another guy I'd been dating for about a month left me in the middle of a movie. Went to get popcorn. Disappeared." She blew at her open palm. "Like David Copperfield. In a puff of smoke."

"You have to be kidding."

A definitive shake of her head. "Not kidding here, Jake. We're talkin' blockbuster dating issues. So I get the whole 'love's not for me' attitude. Easier to take a pass than commit to another round of love and face inevitable heartbreak. Trust me. I. Am. Down. With. That." Her voice dipped to a whisper. "But—and this is what I wanted to tell you." She shifted closer. "This morning? My most recent *company-line package* smashed my heart. *Smashed it.* Like, with a ball-peen hammer." She leaned out of the truck a little farther, her body swinging from the cherry-red door. "But even I know love is out there. And you—you're the expert."

"Ex-expert."

She placed a hand over her heart. "And I—I am the new Kate."

"That's terrific. Now can 'the new Kate' please get in the truck?"

"No. This is important." She shook her head and tried to focus on what he needed to know, but—wow—last martini was really kicking in, or maybe it was the tumble, or the prospect of being stranded, but keeping her thoughts together was tough. "Listen, Jake, you're the guy who wrote the book on great sex. You should be looking for The One, too. Because great sex is part of that package...that whole star-spangled, bells ringing, love-forever package." And her super-sized heart needed that package. The romance, the proposal on bended knee, the everlasting declaration of love. All of it. "I thought my ex was The One, but obviously I was wrong, because The One ponies up the great sex."

"*Really* need you to get back in the truck now."

"Truth be told, my ex wasn't all that and a bag of chips on the old sex-o-meter." She crooked her index finger, and he leaned in. "*If you know what I mean.*"

His eyes narrowed. "Think you might want to change the subject?"

"No, Jake, what I *want* is the chips." Her elbow slipped a few inches down the open door. "Can you tell me where to find The One and some crazy hot chips?"

His hand gripped the doorframe. "Yeah, those martinis are definitely talking."

She tilted closer. "Don't you think I deserve the chips?"

Please say yes.

It wasn't just a sales pitch. She needed to believe it.

He stabbed at his glasses. "Am I really qualified to answer that question?"

"Hell, yes, I deserve the chips." Her fist flew into the air, Norma Rae–style. "*All* women deserve the chips. We all *deserve* the freaking chips."

"Chips for all. That is extremely democratic. Now let's get you back into the truck." He settled her inside the cab, came around, and climbed in the driver's side.

Kate snuggled back against the red leather interior. "Did I tell you I don't like flying?"

"You did."

"And that I might have had a martini or three?"

"You mentioned it, yes." He reached across for her seatbelt and clicked it into place. He *was* a nice guy. He smelled nice, too. Like the deepest blue ocean and fresh salty air.

She closed her eyes and breathed in his scent as her voice drifted away. "Normally, I'm a one martini girl. Two is my night-on-the-town absolute max, but flying a six-seater equipped for an unexpected water landing into the eye of a freaking hurricane scared the hell out of me."

The engine roared into life. "No need to worry now, we're ahead of the weather."

Such a nice, reassuring thing to say. Jake Wright is nice guy. She opened her eyes to sneak a peek as he navigated his F-150 across the narrow runway like a pro. *Nice hands. Nice driving skills.* Maybe he'd be willing to talk about those skills in the impromptu interview. On the QT. A behind-the-closed-doors-of-an-F-series conversation. Play it cool. No mention of love or matchmaking or Smart Cupid.

"So, off the record—"

"One night, no interview." His gaze never left the road.

Kate wrinkled her nose. *Back to his one night, no interview thing.* How could he be so cranky when he was driving a limited edition Super Cab with a six-liter engine?

Well, cranky or not, she refused to give up. Everything was on the line for her, and with just twenty-four hours to score the interview, she planned to make the most of every second.

Take that, Mr. Wright. Mr. Ex-Sex Factor.

She sat up in the comfy seat, opened her tote, and pushed aside two self-help books, her tablet, several highlighters, her phone, keys to her walk-up, the undershirt, and a contractor's license her father had mailed to her last week. When she reached the bottom, she pulled out her voice recorder, pressed the red button, and pointed it in his direction.

Let him try to get her on the next available weather-cleared flight back to Manhattan. This interview was her first real chance to prove she was more than just a pretty girl from Arcadia, and she was going to make it a big, fat, sexy success. *Hurricane or no hurricane.*

Besides, if Jake was honestly through with love, he was in serious trouble—the kind of trouble she knew something about.

Chapter Three

Jake took a sharp right onto the narrow road that led to his cliffside home. Below them, Dante circled offshore, landfall still hours away. Plenty of time to get inside and figure out what the hell he was going to do with Kate Bell until he could hustle her off his island.

"So, which is it—boxers or briefs?"

Jesus. His hands tightened on the steering wheel as he drove alongside the stone coral wall surrounding the property. *Does she really expect me to answer?*

She thrust her recording device toward him, all blond ambition. "Boxers or briefs?"

Apparently she does. "Don't you think that's a little on the personal side?"

Kate released a heavy sigh he interpreted as annoyance. "So much makes sense now."

"What the hell does that mean?" He pulled up to the gate and punched his code into the electronic system.

"The bad attitude. The unwillingness to be interviewed." She looked back at the tablet screen, her forehead wrinkled.

"Definitely a briefs guy."

With his grip fixed on the wheel, he drove through the open gates and parked next to his workshop. "I do not wear briefs."

"Fine—no briefs."

"No briefs." He yanked at his cowlick. Glanced in the rearview. Shook his head.

With his unkempt hair and oversized clothing, he was a perfect facsimile of the brainy middle school kid he'd been, ignored by cheerleaders, reviled by jocks. It was a beautiful thing, or rather, a not-so-beautiful, thing. He'd liked that kid, the young pre-celebrity, unpackaged version of Jake Wright. That kid had dreamed about a woman like the one leaning across the console. The man he'd become turned to look at her, noticing how her jacket had slipped from her shoulder to reveal a silky, camisole-type thing, lacy, probably silk, definitely sexy.

Oh, she was something, all right. Soft green eyes, lit from within and sweet, like an updated 1950s film cutie with a dash of serious sex appeal—a blonde Natalie Wood—all soft curves and sweet Midwestern attitude. A mantrap waiting to happen. Not the tough-talking, flirtatious New Yorker he'd expected, but a definite mantrap. A real pleasure for the eyes. Unlike her persistence, which was decidedly unpleasant.

"So you sport the other ones, those cute…you know…" she said, tapping the side of her tablet, "those cute…briefy boxery kind."

Briefy boxery kind? Seriously? Hell, next she'd be asking what size jock strap he wore. He slammed the truck into park. "There's no way in hell I'm going to answer that question."

"Ooh-kay, then." She typed into an app on her tablet. *COMMANDO.*

Jake slipped the keys from the ignition, stared out the windshield, and tried to not to lose his shit. "No, I do not go commando, I'm not interested in love, matchmaking, or being paraded around Smart Cupid's website, wearing a pair of star-spangled boxer shorts. Period. End."

There was a short pause. "Well, if you don't answer…"

"Fine." He banged his palms against the steering wheel. "Boxer briefs. Or briefy boxers. Whatever you called them. Jesus, who cares what type of underwear a guy owns?"

She typed *boxer briefs*, then backspaced over it and re-typed *commando*. "I liked you better when you were *au naturel*."

"I was never *au naturel*." He spared a quick, irritated glance at her phone. "You can't answer the questions for me. Seriously, what kind of journalist are you?" *The drunken kind. The cute kind. The kind who is messing with my peaceful existence.*

She let out an exasperated sigh. "The kind who needs answers. Give me *something*."

"Fine." He gritted his teeth. Literally gritted his teeth. "I prefer Coke to Pepsi."

She batted her pretty eyelashes. "And do you prefer brunettes to redheads?"

"No, actually, I like blondes."

Her eyes narrowed. "Blonde was not an option."

"You wanted to know, Miss Bell."

Her eyes narrowed further, although he hadn't believed further narrowing was possible. "Please, *please*, call me Kate." She jabbed at the application window multiple times. "*Kate, Kate, Kate*. Honestly, if we're going to be sharing your blonde, Coca-Cola fantasies, a first-name basis seems appropriate."

He kept his hands safely on the wheel. "Except we're *not* going to be sharing my blonde, Coca-Cola fantasies. Not that I have any blonde, Coca-Cola fantasies, but if I did, we wouldn't be sharing them. Once the storm passes, I'm booking you a flight straight back to Manhattan."

She stared up at him from beneath those lashes, undeterred. "Sexting—twenty-first century turn-on or new-fangled invitation to trouble?"

His forehead dropped to the steering wheel. She was relentless. "No comment."

"Not commenting isn't an option. The women of Smart Cupid want to know details about the bachelor. Secret fantasies. Preferences."

A low growl formed in the back of this throat. *Typical.* His ex-wife had exhibited preferences. She'd *preferred* his literary agent. No wonder he hadn't written a book in three years. "Smart Cupid can kiss my—"

"All I want to do is ask you a few questions. Once I get your basic stats, likes and dislikes, we can move on to examining your expertise. You have so much advice to offer Smart Cupid's readers on building strong, lovable relationships—"

"Strong *love* relationships."

"Yes, exactly." She stabbed at the air. "Strong love relationships. By a factor of sex."

Man, she was tipsy. Bold, too, referencing the title of his book, but also determined, accident-prone, funny, and completely adorable. *Insanely* adorable.

He cracked a self-mocking smile. Minus the vodka, exactly his type—when he used to have a type. He hadn't had any type for a year, eighteen months. Shoving the unwelcome knowledge out of his mind, he threw open the door of the truck and climbed out. "No interview. One night."

"But—"

He closed the door on her protest. One minute of peace, that's all he wanted, one minute to regroup and get a hold of his thoughts.

At the back of the truck, he untied the tarp and hoisted her bag out of the flatbed. A pink duffle bag. Honestly, what kind of woman carried a pink duffle? He slung the damn thing over his shoulder and walked around the truck, intent on keeping himself together until she was safely on a plane back to Manhattan, but as he reached the passenger side, his gaze locked onto a feminine set of legs dangling outside the door.

Damn—seriously? She leaned forward, and his attention shifted north from her slim ankles to her rockin' curves and the inlet of her waist. Framed by the red door, all rounded and sweet-looking, blonde curls tumbling over her shoulders, she was exactly his type. He pressed his glasses against the bridge of his nose. *Oh yeah, Miss Ohio could definitely break me.*

He leaned in to pull an extra flashlight from the glove box. She smelled good, too, an optimistic blend of liquid soap and cherry blossoms. The last thing he needed was optimism. Between her true confessions about chips and sex-o-meters, and her off-the-charts commando commentary, he was already fighting a headache. Her brand of optimism was a luxury he couldn't afford. Better to deal with reality. His ex-wife had taught him that. Then again, she'd never smelled like cherry blossoms. Man, he loved cherry blossoms. He dug through his pockets for the keys.

Good thing he was famous for his self-control. But watching her climb from the passenger seat, noting how the movement caused her skirt to ride a bit higher up on her thighs, an unexpected hit of desire shot through his veins. *The hell with the keys. The hell with the hurricane.*

Dammit, what was wrong with him? He slammed the brakes on his thoughts. No matter how enjoyable it was to look at Kate Bell, he was in a definite look—don't touch—situation.

Thunder rumbled overhead, and as raindrops started to fall, she dashed toward the wraparound porch. He followed behind her, moving through the rain, the gravel driveway crunching beneath his feet. She waited as he unlocked the door, leaning her curves against a latticed railing dripping with bougainvillea, the flowers bending in the wind. Her body swayed along with the bright blooms. And if the leaning was amazing, the sway was fantastic.

With more effort than he cared to admit, Jake pulled his gaze away from her tipsy, seductive form and opened the heavy door of his gray saltbox bungalow. His home was one of the original houses on the island, and he'd restored it piece by piece with found wood and vintage hardware, everything from the widow's walk to the wide-plank floors that led to the French doors and out the stone steps to Lovers Beach.

Jake flipped the wall switch. Light flooded the hard slate tile of the entry. Still had power, which was a good sign. He glanced around as he always did and felt the familiar contentment at the center of his soul. He loved this place, hidden from the rest of the island. Maybe the only place he felt at home now. And Kate Bell, well...she swayed into the place as if she and his bungalow formed a perfect match.

He watched her take in the dark floors, the peaked, turreted ceilings, and the oversized stone fireplace. Built along the cliff, the place could seem as much a fortress as a bungalow.

"Interesting place," she said.

Jake set down her overstuffed bag, took off his glasses, and wiped the rain from the lenses with the hem of his shirt. "Thanks, I still have some work to do."

It'd been a long time since he'd invited a woman into his bed, or rather, his home, and suddenly, the place felt significantly smaller. *And much less empty.*

Ignoring his thoughts, he shoved his glasses back on, picked up the duffle, and strode through the entry into the house. Kate trailed behind him, shoes in hand, her bare feet quiet against the tile. A collection of gray clouds created shadows over the skylights of the beamed ceilings, and the rain pressed hard against the wall of windows at the back of the house.

"Nice work on the tongue-and-groove hardwoods."

His head swiveled in the direction of her voice. "Excuse me?"

"Tough to match the original floors in a restoration." Her pink painted toes drew an invisible semi-circle on the polished wood. "You did a good job."

"Thanks," he said, surprised and pleased to have his handiwork appreciated.

She crisscrossed the floor, moving unsteadily toward the fireplace. "Strong effort on the mantle and the marble facing here, too. Did you install the French doors?"

Hypnotized by the sashay of her hips and her amazing knowledge of home restoration, he blinked his way back to the bungalow. "Yeah…I did."

Head tilted to the side, she said, "See, there. At the bottom of the piston travel, if you install that up against the door the way you have it, the door won't close properly." She grabbed a leveler from the open toolbox next to the fireplace. Not sure tools and martinis mixed, he stepped toward her, but she swiveled by and walked to the doors. "Put more tension on the piston, bring the stop out a quarter of an inch past the groove, and the door will be in better opposition with the closer." She tossed him a crazy-cute smile. "Rookie mistake."

Jake ran a hand over his jaw and considered her surprisingly sound advice.

"Take a lookie here," she continued, waving the leveler dangerously close to the hinge. "The speed adjustment screw at the end of the closer allows you to adjust how fast the door closes. If the door is closing too fast, jus' tighten up the screw. If you need more speed, loosen the screw 'til you've got it right."

Speed. Tighten. Screw.

She leaned against the doorjamb, all inadvertent seduction, and his effort to avoid picturing her wearing nothing but his tool belt failed.

Drunk, he reminded himself.

Hands off.

He cleared his throat. "Where did you learn…?"

"My dad owns a construction firm back in Arcadia, built it from the ground up. I'm an only child, so he wants me back in Ohio running the company." Her shoulder shrugged against the doorjamb. "*Katie Bell Construction*, named after me and built by my dad's own workmanlike hands. His dream." She stared down at her pink toes. "I wish it were mine."

He nodded. "Explains the whole 'stuck in Ohio' comment."

Kate slanted him a look. "So you *were* listening."

"You don't want the job?"

An uncertain expression worried her pretty features. "I don't want to hurt him."

Another nod. He shoved his hands deep into the pockets of his rain-spattered chinos and offered a teasing smile. "I bet you look cute in a hard hat."

She wrinkled her nose. "Let's just say yellow's not my color."

"Aw, I bet you look cute in yellow." After an awkward silence, he jerked his chin toward the front windows. "I need to finish installing the storm shutters, so…" He indicated an archway that led to the bedrooms. "Bedrooms are that way. If you need to get into some dry clothes."

"Or I could help board up the windows. Prepare for the storm?"

Jake gave her a dubious look. She was cute, but there was no way he trusted her with a power tool after three martinis. "Maybe you should take a nap, sleep off the vodka."

"You mean the Russian courage." She peeled her body

away from the door, tripped toward him, and handed over the leveler. "Maybe you're right. Probably too tipsy for general contracting," she said, winding her way toward the archway.

Yeah, she's tipsy, all right.

And sweet.

And sexy.

And so not what I expected.

He set the tools on the mantle and followed her zigzagging form toward the bedrooms.

Halfway down the hall, she unbuttoned her suit jacket and slipped it off her shoulders, revealing a lacy camisole-type thing that nudged his natural reserve along a dangerous road.

"Ya know what, Jake?" A laugh bubbled up from her chest, and the sound was so out of the blue, so adorable, it stopped him in his tracks. "I bet you'd look cute in a hard hat, too. Not all brooding and sexy and hot, like the pathologically vain, run-of-the-nightclub types I have vowed to avoid..." She swayed farther to the left and tossed a wink at him over her shoulder. "But cute. *Definitely* cute."

And that's when it hit him.

Of all the trouble his sister had dished out in the years since his divorce, sending this woman to Paradise Cay was the kind of trouble that might just bring him to his knees.

Chapter Four

Kate opened her eyes, a simple effort that made her moan miserably, so she let her lids drift shut and burrowed back into her pillow. Or, wait a second—*was* this her pillow? Her eyes flew open. These were definitely not her dark gray sheets, and wait…why was she smelling aftershave? She bit down on her bottom lip. Maybe because this was *not* her bed. *Where the hell am I?*

She sat up, and the quick movement sent a shot of unexpected pain through her skull. *Okay, no more quick movements.* She pressed her palm to her forehead and inched back against the headboard. *Slow and steady.* Her eyes narrowed on the pink duffle resting on a trunk at the end of the bed. Her tote bag on the right. Kitten heels neatly to the left—but they were broken. Her face crumpled. *Why are they broken?* She stared at the shoes as the tiny ball-peen hammer in her head chipped away at a few vague recollections, until… suddenly, everything rushed back.

The breakup.

The meltdown.

The flight from hell.

The martinis.

Oh God. Her eyes slammed shut.

The martinis.

Never indulge in more than one martini. That was her rule. Now as broken as her kitten heels. Worse, after breaking said rule, she'd gone and stumbled drunkenly into her boss's brother. Literally stumbled into him. Drunk. *Oh God.* The room spun wildly in some unseen axis as she remembered...

Colliding into him. Climbing into his truck. Babbling about her ex being gorgeous but not a bag of chips, and then... she covered her face with both hands.

Declaring I deserve the chips.

A humiliated moan escaped her. Chip-talking with Jake Wright. The chips *expert.* Her hands slid down her face. And something else... Had he mentioned *democracy*? And had she responded with *orgasms for everyone*?

Or maybe she'd only thought it. "Please, God, let me only have thought it."

If not, just strike me down now.

She tried to ignore the pounding at her temples, but it was tough. Bed-headed, cotton-mouthed, and wishing she'd downloaded that stress management app before she'd left her apartment this morning, three things became appallingly clear: olives were not a breakfast food, martinis were *not* one of the four major food groups, and she'd never drink vodka again. *Never.* The bottle should come with a warning label.

On a sigh, she lifted the strap of her camisole onto her shoulder and reminded herself that facing her mistakes was an important part of the growth and self-actualization process. *Today is simply a growth opportunity*, she thought, glancing at the boarded-up windows. It was so dark. What time was it? A quick glance at her cell told her she'd been napping. She never *napped*. Of course, she never drank more than one vodka martini, either. A knock on the door startled her, sending her heart leaping into her throat. Her entire body burned hot and tingly, and not in the good way, more in the panic attack way. She pulled the sheet up to her chin, beyond mortified. "Come in."

The door opened as if in slow motion, revealing her reluctant host, now clad in a pair of low-slung gray sweatpants and a faded graphic tee. His feet were bare. His hair was damp, longish, curling into the back of his neck. His glasses were different, too. He'd traded the protective eye gear for a sleeker pair of hipster frames. Still unshaven. Scruffy. But cute. Definitely, *definitely* cute. An inkling shuffled its way from the back of her mind. Had she told him that? Oh my God, had she *winked*?

A smile tugged at the corners of his mouth. "Hey."

Oh yeah, she'd told him.

"Hey." Would the humiliation never end?

He cleared her throat and held out the tray. "Not sure what works for you, so I brought everything. Black coffee, microwaved pancakes, my family's special hangover concoction. And Tylenol." He stepped into the room and set her options carefully on the nightstand.

Kate eyed what looked like a tomato juice smoothie with a stalk of celery poking out of the glass and attempted a smile as tiny little hammers intensified their clobbering of her temples. "Does it work? The family recipe?"

His eyes shuttered behind the thick lenses, suddenly guarded. "Never tried it myself. More my father's territory, really."

"Oh." She reached awkwardly for the Tylenol. Rumor had it his father had been more interested in gambling and drinking than his family. Her parents called every Sunday, rain, shine, or Buckeye football. Hard to imagine being left by them. *Maybe that's why he doesn't believe in love.* She turned the plastic bottle over in her palm. "This is perfect, thank you."

Hands buried in the pockets of his sweats, he nodded. "You might want to clean up and change. Winds will be getting high, so a power outage is likely." His gaze fell briefly to where the sheet had pulled away to reveal the torn seam of her skirt, and he turned away as if the sight of her red panties burned his retinas. His chin jerked toward the door to the right of the boarded windows. "Everything you need is in the connecting bathroom."

"Thank you," she said, adjusting the sheet.

He offered an efficient nod. "Storm regulations prevent showering, but I boiled some water, let it cool, and set it out on the sink with soap and fresh towels."

The slow crawl of a blush burned across her skin. Part of her was touched he'd taken the time to ensure she had what she needed, especially after she'd drunkenly crash-landed in his bed. Such a thoughtful thing to do, so *nice*. The other part imagined spending the night here, in this boarded-up bungalow, in the midst of the storm, with a man who was a virtual stranger sleeping a few feet away in the next room, and the intimacy felt…honestly, she didn't know what she felt.

"Probably best to leave and let you get ready." He reached into the pocket of his pants and pulled out a flashlight with her name on it. Literally. Masking tape. A Sharpie. And her fate written on a Fenix TK60. "We'll definitely be stuck here for the night."

Kate accepted the flashlight and attempted a smile.

Stuck here.

For the night.

• • •

Fifteen minutes and three Tylenol later, a clean, refreshed Kate focused the beam of the flashlight on the note tucked inside her pre-packed bag. A white envelope emblazoned with a mischievous Cupid taking aim from atop a lacy, black nightie. She slipped the card from the envelope and recognized Jane's distinctive handwriting immediately. Her eyes scanned the message written across the heavy linen cardstock. *When in Paradise…*

Kate tightened the knotted towel at her chest and surveyed the room with its hurricane panels, neutral colors, and hard masculine furniture. Not exactly paradise. Especially when combined with the words "stuck here for the night."

A pit formed in her stomach, and she rifled through the bag's brightly-colored contents.

Bikini. Bikini. Thong bikini. Bikini. Strappy sundress. Bikini. Sarong. She hooked a pinky through the skimpy string-top and wrinkled her nose at the so-called clothing. *Not the business casual layers she'd been expecting, but with nudity as her other option…*

She dropped the bikini and unzipped a second, smaller compartment, but the pickings were even slimmer. Lacy underwear. Shortie pajamas adorned with a smattering of bawdy conversation hearts.

How was she supposed to face him, wearing pajamas covered in hearts that said, *I Prefer My Valentines Naked* and *All Night Long?* The only other items in the bag were a pair of sparkly sandals and this month's hottest romance novel. Yep, her friend was definitely playing matchmaker.

An annoyed crease formed between her brows. Jake Wright was not her type. Besides, he was her ticket to *Cosmo*, to a life in NYC, a chance to build her dreams despite expectation. No more. No less. She glanced back at the pink duffle. When she got back to the city, she was going to put her friend through the ringer. Although, in all honesty, it had been *her* idea to jumpstart the new Kate. Several hours ago, the thought of a short-term romance had sounded…well, better than heartbroken.

But now she was *here*.

Naked.

With nothing to wear but a towel, a bikini, or the frayed white tee hidden at the bottom of her tote. She reached for the bag, pushed aside a copy of *The Sex Factor* she'd picked up at the airport and pulled out the shirt. The cotton was irritatingly appealing. Just like her ex, enticing on the surface but empty on the inside. She'd torch it, but a three-alarm fire was not what she needed. What she needed was therapy.

She marched into the adjoining bathroom, splashed some water on her face, and wiped up the sink basin with the shirt. She never wanted to see it again. Never wanted to hear the words "Fruit of the Loom." In fact, if she never saw another piece of fruit, it would be too soon.

Kate tossed the T-shirt into the trash, sat down on top of the toilet, and let her head sink between her knees. This breakup had been coming for a while. There'd been signs. Nights when he'd come home late. Unreturned texts. Less time spent together. *Frayed at the edges.*

She pressed her fingers to the dulling ache behind her eyes and drew in a breath on the count of seven. On the exhale, she picked up her phone from the spot on the granite counter where she'd left it and typed out a text to Jane.

Remind me NOT to let you pack my bag for my NEXT vacation.

Not a bad conversation starter. A quick tap on the send button and... *Your text cannot be delivered.* No power. No cell service.

Obviously, she'd have to deal with her friend later. Right now, she needed to focus on the positives. Despite the hurricane that was knocking down power lines, she was in Paradise. And despite his reluctance, Jake Wright was a major get. Three years ago, everyone had wanted an interview with him. Then he'd disappeared. Vanished. Into the salty ocean air.

Now he was right outside her door.

No headache or slinky sundress was going to stand in her way.

Kate stared at her reflection in the glass shower door and repeated her mantra. "Skills, success…*confidence.*"

Except she needed more than mere confidence. She needed heavy artillery, some kind of advantage to win him over and convince him to sign on as her bachelor.

Something like…his book.

She opened the bathroom door with the tip of her toe, just enough to spy her open tote. Inside that bag lay secrets. Jake Wright's secrets. She'd never actually read her bachelor's bestseller. Sure, she knew the title — who didn't? But she didn't know his secrets. She'd bet her fanny there were some insights between those paperback covers. Maybe she needed to do a little research. Find out what made her reluctant bachelor tick.

She snuck a peek at the tray he'd so sweetly provided, and a small knot of guilt formed in her throat. Jake Wright may be a sex expert, but he was also an Eagle Scout, first rank. Prepared. Responsible. Equipped for an emergency like a tipsy bedmate.

Probably saw a lot of those types of emergencies, she thought, following the beam of her flashlight across the tile floor and into the bedroom. She stared down at the pink duffle, her conscience forcing her to rethink her research plan. Less than two hours spent in his company and Kate already knew he wouldn't like the idea. But if he refused to answer her questions or give her any insight into his romantic desires, what choice did she have? Research was part of her job. She needed to find a way to crack open that non-believing heart of his, and if he refused to budge…well, all's fair in war and matchmaking.

She lifted the book from the bag and aimed the flashlight at the back cover. No author photo. No bio. She flipped to the front pages.

Copyright? Three years ago. Her mouth quirked to one side. Same as when he left New York. Hard to believe that was coincidental. She turned to the start of the book.

Chapter One: Rules of Seduction.

That pesky knot of guilt moved from her throat to her chest, and she drew in a determined breath. *Don't back off now, Katie. Do your job. Research his seduction strategies and convince him to be* Smart Cupid's *Man Candy Crush of the Month.* Like Nike said, *just do it.*

Propping the book up on the pillow, she stacked up a few of the bikinis and wedged them underneath the Fenix so the light shone on the list of sexy rules.

1. Be Spontaneous.

Her gaze slid to her duffle bag and she hooked the sundress—the only reasonable clothing option available—with her index finger. The deep curve of its neckline and the bold floral pattern seemed pretty spontaneous, especially considering that if she had her way she'd be wearing a navy pencil skirt. She stepped into the dress, wriggled the fabric over her hips and settled the thin straps on her shoulders. Damn thing fit her like a glove. Made her wonder how long her friend had been planning the "spontaneous" ambush. She sat on the bed, curled her bare feet under her hip, and kept reading.

2. Master The Perfect Kiss.

3. Pillow Talk (What turns her on?)

4. Learn Your Partner's Secrets.

How many times had she wished her ex would take the time to learn what turned her on? Greet her in a bubble bath surrounded by scented candles, rather than on the couch in the living room, remote clued into reality television? Hell, she would've stripped naked, climbed into the tub, and let the water splash over the side while she seduced him into a mad frenzy. Not that the situation was one of her intimate secret fantasies. But a night like that might just... Her throat went dry as she read the next sexy, little rule. A night like that might just...

5. Blow. Her. Mind.

Eyes glued to the promise of those words, Kate adjusted the straps of her sundress in an effort to distract herself from the sexy hum building inside her body. Clearly, the book had been a bestseller for a reason. After a quick glance at the door, she turned the page and read the next words aloud, her voice a near-whisper. "Embrace your shared moments of humanity and laughter, your partner's imperfections, and her playfulness—that's where the sexual magic lives. Invest in her as a person, show deeper interest. It's not about the sex. The sex is only one factor. It's about knowing who she is." Barely breathing, she closed the book.

Yowza.

Kate had known she'd gain some insight into Jake from reading his book, but she never bargained on feeling seduced by his romantic, sexy words. But she had been. Seduced. And now, more than ever, she needed to know how the man who'd written this list had become the man who refused to believe in love. Because from what she'd just read, not only did this man believe in The One, but he'd treasure every inch of her.

And what woman doesn't want that?

Chapter Five

Jake wasn't sure when, or if, the hurricane would hit landfall, or how long the storm might last, but he'd prepared as if they'd be facing the apocalypse. Growing up in a situation that felt like the bottom might drop at any minute had made him a guy who prepared. Lots of folks gave him a hard time for being rigid, emotionally distant, always seeking perfection, but he felt more grounded when everything was in order. Dealing with a father who bullied his family over a lost hoodie or a late dinner made a kid grow up fast. Shut down fast, too.

He gave his preparations the once-over. Boarded up, the living room fell dark without the electricity, lit only by two hurricane lamps and the candles he'd set out in mason jars on every table and in the fireplace. He was surprised by the effect. If he hadn't uttered the words "stuck here all night" the upshot might have been romantic. Not that he was aiming for romance. He most certainly was not. But *stuck here all night*? Not the most generous way to frame the situation, even if he hadn't been expecting an overnight guest. Especially not one with a set of curves and legs that wouldn't quit.

Suddenly claustrophobic, he pulled at his crewneck and shoved aside the disarming thoughts. His brusque words and uncomfortable feelings had nothing to do with Kate Bell or her idealized notions about soulmates and outspoken desire for perfect sex.

Perfect sex. The words were still echoing through his brain when he heard the soft footfalls of bare feet against the hardwood. He turned to see her approaching the fireplace, following a path lit by the glow of her flashlight. The room's shadows played across her face. She was beautiful, straight up, pin-up girl gorgeous, all curvy and blonde. Clad in a killer red dress with barely-there straps and a sheer skirt, she was like a vision out of a man's dreams.

His dreams.

But there was something else. Something she'd said earlier rang in his ears. *"Don't give me the sweetheart treatment."* As if she was judged on her femininity more than she liked. Jake suspected there was more to her than beauty—although there was a helluva lot of that going on. But more, too. Intelligence. Determination. A kind heart. He was curious, more so than he'd been about a woman in a long time.

"Hey."

"Hey." He swallowed hard and gestured toward the floor. "Ready to ride out the storm?"

In a spot away from the unprotected skylights, he'd set up a makeshift camp next to the fireplace. Bottled water, a stack of sandwiches, a Thermos of coffee, an open game of Scrabble, a few other board games, and a battery-operated radio. Plus, all kinds of snacks.

Kate wrapped both arms around her chest in a sweet, protective gesture that inadvertently enhanced the whole pin-up girl view. "Looks like we've got enough supplies for a week."

Jake nodded his acknowledgment and looked away. Hell,

he was only human. He cleared his throat. "Never hurts to be prepared. And Scrabble is…"

"The best board game ever."

"Love Scrabble." He pinned her with a look. "But I'm competitive. Don't go easy on me."

A smile tugged at the edges of her mouth. "I'll keep that in mind."

"Hungry?" he asked.

"Thank you," she said, their words overlapping. "I am… hungry." She drew in a breath and handed him the pain reliever. "And…I'm also really sorry."

He held up the bottle. "For emptying my Tylenol supply?"

"No, I mean…" Still wrapped in that protective gesture, she looped her index finger inside the tiny red strap at her shoulder. "I'm sorry about my behavior."

Jake tried to concentrate, but his gaze kept drifting to her shoulder. He'd been in a sex-free zone for longer than he cared to admit. Concentration was tough. "Your behavior?"

"Earlier. On the tarmac. In the hallway." She let out a long sigh. "The martinis and the winking and the less-than-appropriate questions."

He waved her off. "You don't need to worry about anything. Do you feel better?"

"Yes, I do." Kate shifted her weight from one foot to the other. "Or I *would* if we could forget everything I said about my ex and the whole star-spangled sex thing…" Her words drifted off in a mixture of desperation and hope.

"Yeah, that'll be difficult." Jake smiled, amused by her obvious chagrin. "And, not to get too personal, but I *think* your point was that the sex was *less* than star-spangled."

A charming pink blush colored her cheeks. "Yes."

"No worries. All's forgotten." He set the plastic bottle on the mantle above the fireplace. "Pain officially killed."

She smiled over at him. He returned the smile and took a

step back. Then another. Kate Bell was a love blogger sent to fuck up his peaceful world. He needed to remember that. But damned if he could keep from smiling.

She nodded at the radio. "Any news?"

Putting more distance between them, Jake picked up the battery-operated radio. "Only one way to find out." He flipped on the power, tuned to the AM frequency, and dialed through the interference to a local emergency station.

A series of high pitched sounds preceded the start of the announcement. *"According to the Caribbean Oceanic & Atmospheric Center, Dante has been downgraded from a Category 1 hurricane to a tropical storm. Atmospheric conditions associated with El Niño have made it difficult for hurricanes to develop this season and Dante will be no exception. Nevertheless, island officials ask people to remain vigilant and indoors."*

The broadcaster delivered additional news and instructions in an easy islander accent. But no crisis data, no evacuation order. "Sounds like we're going to get lucky."

Her eyes widened comically at the edges. "Oh yeah?"

"Not that kind of lucky," he teased. "But it does sound like we're not going anywhere tonight." He tuned in to the classic blues station and eased onto the faux fur blanket next to the stone hearth. Once settled, he placed a sandwich and a single serving bag of Sunchips onto a paper plate. "Not exactly five star, but…"

"Thank you." Accepting his no-cook, emergency-style meal, she took a seat next to him on the blanket. Close, but not too close. The room grew quiet, save the wind whistling outside the paneled windows. He ripped open his chips.

She cleared her throat. Took a bite of the sandwich. "This is good. Better than my usual Friday afternoon splurge at the deli on 4th and Lex." She made a sound of appreciation that had him wishing he'd meant the other kind of lucky, but he'd be a damned fool if he gave in to *that* kind of thought. She plainly wanted—*needed*—love and romance, the whole package he couldn't give. Except her mouth was so inviting. And her neck... But then she said, "Do you ever miss New York?"

And—boom. Just like that, he felt the immediate shutdown of his expression. His self-imposed exile from New York was a personal topic and a great place to start an interview. He drew in a breath and tried to stay cool. "Part of Smart Cupid's company line?"

"What? No. I only meant..." Her words trailed off, and he waited silently, hoping to be wrong, hoping he wasn't being played. "From what I can tell, you've been away a long while, and I know what that's like. To be away from your family. Away from home."

The muscles in his jaw clenched. The subject of home and family was as off-limits as his boxer briefs. "And yet, you're not in Ohio."

She set down her plate, not looking at him as she straightened. "No, I'm not."

"Why not?" He watched her from across the blanket as the sound of the rainfall against the skylights reverberated between them. Time to put the love blogger in the hot seat.

Her response was quiet but certain. "Because I need to be my own person."

Surprised by her candor, he pressed for more. "And how is that different than me?"

Still avoiding his gaze, she continued. "Because unlike you, I've never been taken seriously, and I want to be." She moved the plate in a circle, clockwise. "But until my dad can go into the Arcadia grocery store and hold my by-lined, full-colored copy in his hands, well, to him, to my whole family, I'll just be the dream-filled girl wasting her time in New York, when I should be home, running the business."

A bitter sound formed in the back of his throat. "Being taken seriously isn't all it's cracked up to be."

Her next softly spoken words were a challenge. "Well, at least I'm not hiding."

"And I am?" He hated the sudden cynicism in his voice, but living through the fallout of that damned book, not to mention his marriage, had killed some deep-rooted part of him. "Is that the theory my sister is currently floating? Or are you just another woman who's read the book and feels like she knows me?"

Her eyes flashed, stormy as the skies outside. "Who says I read your book?"

The muscles tightened in his jaw. "By a 'factor of sex,'" he said, adding air quotes as a reminder. "A few hours ago you were citing the damn thing. Or was that the martinis talking?"

She winced. "Knowing the *title* of your bestseller isn't exactly 'citing the damn thing,'" she said, throwing in a set of air quotes for good measure. "Why are you being so defensive?"

"Defensive?" He jumped on her words, not believing for a second she wasn't working an angle for her interview. He stabbed at his glasses. "You really expect me to believe you don't know?"

"Know what?"

"About my marriage, my career…the blowback from the whole mess." Her reply was a simple shake of her head. "Well, you are one in a million."

He ran a hand over the stubble on his chin, drifting back in time. *The Sex Factor* had hit all the lists. He'd made it. He was successful. Out of Brooklyn. Best time of his life. Blessed with a great marriage—or so he'd thought—a strong, respectable counseling practice and a commercial literary triumph that would've allowed him to focus on serious psychological study, he was flying high. And then—bam—all of it, gone.

Overnight he'd become the relationship therapist with the cheating wife. He remembered the humiliation, the professional embarrassment. Rather than stay in New York, he'd taken the money left after the divorce and bought the island. A year later, he built the resort, a place for couples to get away from all the bullshit, to rediscover love. But not him. Never him.

Had he ever been able to feel that way? He wanted to think so. But if he ever had been able to, he couldn't anymore. Not now. He was broken.

"If you want to talk…" He shook away his thoughts and watched her absently moving a few tiles around the Scrabble board. "Off the record."

"Off the record?"

She offered a small smile. A short nod. Stacked up a few game tiles.

Damn. She was sweet, and he hadn't talked, *really* talked, with anyone in… "*Off the record*, my ex is the reason I came to Paradise. To get away from the media circus of my divorce." *Forget the promises thrown back in my face.*

Hell, even standing at the altar in his monkey suit, he'd felt uneasy, unsettled. Fashion shows and the Grammys were held in Gotham Hall, not weddings. Not his kind anyway. He'd wanted St. Brigid's in the East Village, but the 19th century church wasn't built to accommodate the four-hundred strangers gathered to wish him well. His ex had always been more interested in his celebrity than in him. He'd simply failed to notice.

He felt a sharp pain in his chest, like his heart flinched. Yeah, he'd felt like something was missing with his ex. But she'd seemingly adored him. His instincts had told him that whatever was missing, they'd figure it out. They'd build it. Together. Forever.

Wrong. Wrong in every single way.

How could he trust his instincts again?

The room grew quiet except for the wind, the rain, the *click-clack* of letter tiles rising in a tower at the edge of the board. Kate sighed. "My ex, the one who fit the company-line package to a T, emptied out his side of the closet and left me with a box of donuts."

Jake made a sound at the back of his throat. So she'd had it rough, too. "Not a nice guy."

"No," she said in a soft, faraway voice. "Not a nice guy."

Stupid jackass. His mouth twisted to one side. "Mine slept with my agent, or rather, my ex-agent, all while I was building my career as an authority on romantic relationships." He rubbed at the back of his neck, not quite believing he'd told her. "Didn't exactly make me look like an expert."

"Ouch."

"Yeah — ouch."

Thinking about it made his teeth ache. Maybe he was hiding, but fighting it out in New York had felt impossible. Even now, the last thing he wanted to do was respond to his ex-agent's calls demanding that he get back to the city and stand by his commitment to a second book. What a joke. Jake could terminate the damn contract based on the little known who-can-write-a-book-for-an-asshole clause. If there wasn't such a clause, well, for fuck's sake, there ought to be. He scrubbed his face with both hands.

Kate cleared his throat before saying, "So your wife — "

"Ex-wife."

"Ex-wife." She met his gaze with what felt like a combination of empathy and surprise. Empathy, courtesy of the fact that she'd experienced a recent love disaster, and surprise that he'd revealed something so personal. "So she didn't love you the right way. That doesn't need to make you cynical. Not forever anyway. You've got to know what you wrote is amazing."

Jake slanted his gaze in her direction. "So you admit you've read it?"

"No. Yes. Part of it." She picked up a bottle of water, opened it and took a swallow. "I may have bought a new copy on the way to the airport."

He raised his brows above the glasses. "A new copy?"

"Let's just say, this was a last minute assignment. I'm only here because…long story, short…it might be the only way to save my career."

"Since I'm not going to do the interview…" He gave her a smile that let her know he was no longer completely averse to the idea. "What's your backup plan?"

She snapped the strap of the sundress. "Oh, I brought plenty of things for a backup plan."

He kept his expression neutral. "The dress?"

"Definitely the dress." She laid down tiles for the word "BIKINIS" in the center of the board. "Maybe even a few bikinis…"

"Bikinis, huh?"

"*Several* bikinis, actually." She laughed and tilted her head toward the board. "Twenty-six points. Double word score."

Jake nodded, amused, and a little impressed by her game. Not to mention her laugh. Man, she had a great laugh. "So you're here to save your career and get over your ex?"

She gave him a sidelong glance. "Not *necessarily* in that order."

He nodded. *Interesting.* "Career versus love. The age-old question."

LOVE. She built the word on the edge the board. "Not much of a question for me. I always go into a relationship looking for love." She shrugged. "Maybe that's my problem."

"What's the alternative?"

"What's the alternative?"

"To love?" She blushed a pretty pink that had him

wondering how far past the edge of her sexy dress that sweet blush extended. "Take things as they come."

Man did he want to see where a kiss with her could lead. But that was stupid. She wasn't here for that. Certainly not from him.

Right?

"So you're not here for a relationship?"

She chewed on her bottom lip, which only made him want to kiss her more. "I know that's what I want. One day. But maybe forgetting about that for a while is what I need for now. Thinking it's time for something different. Spontaneous."

He'd kill for that to be true. "You sure about that?"

"Hard to say. I've never done that sort of thing." Another glance up from beneath those lashes. "Just forgotten about the future and jumped a guy." Her voice had gone low. Become sultry. Irresistible. "First time for everything, right?"

"First time." *First time in a long time. Not smart. Not smart at all.* He cracked open a bottle of water, hoping it would cool down his thoughts. "What else do you write for Smart Cupid? Besides the Man Candy Crush of the Month."

"You mean, besides the *bachelor profile*," she said, her tone laced with teasing reproach. "I write a daily blog about the dating scene in Manhattan. Modern Love. Relationships."

"Ah, relationships," he repeated, raising the water bottle in a mock toast.

"With a capital R." Her fingers sifted through the letters, adding the R-word to the game. "But there's room for other possibilities, too." She offered a smile. "Flirtations. Passions. I blog about everything. Friday Night Love Bingo at the Brooklyn fire station. Speed dating in Tribeca. No topic is off-limits." She tucked a blonde curl behind her ear, a gesture he found oddly endearing. "Last week, we featured an online quiz about finding his passion threshold."

"His passion threshold?"

She gave a short nod. "Defines how much passion a man can handle." A smile played at the edges of her mouth. "Want to give it a shot?" He cocked an eyebrow, and she clarified, "The *quiz*."

"Right. The quiz." He leaned back on his elbows, legs crossed at the ankles. "Tonight's off the record, so…why not?" Might not fall into the wise category, but if it meant a chance to flip the tables and define *her* threshold, gain insight into *her* limits, he was all in.

Her smile widened. "Okay…first question."

She tilted her head in thought, and the simple movement exposed her curves in a way that made focusing on her quiz next to impossible. "Let's see, the first question was…"

He felt captivated—that's how he felt. Captivated by her curves, her smile, the way the velvety hum of her voice echoed the pulse of the rain. How long had it been since he'd noticed a woman for *any* reason, much less for the tone of her voice or the fabulousness of her curves?

"Favorite type of music. Classical, rock'n roll, elevator, or rhythm & blues?"

He looked over and caught her gaze. She smiled back at him. *Damn. Totally captivated.* "Gotta be rhythm & blues… soulful, slow, sexy…that's the way I like it." He heard the soft breath hitch in her throat, and suddenly, he was smiling, too. Maybe he wasn't the only one feeling the strange electricity building between them. "What about you? What's your favorite?"

"I'm the one asking the questions, remember?"

"I don't recall any restrictions on the quiz."

She opened her mouth—probably to debate the quiz-taking rules—but stopped and said simply, "Fine. Classic rock."

He gave a slow nod of approval. "Loud and bold. I like it."

She pinned him with a look. "Next question—movie

genre. Mystery, Comedy, Thriller, or Action."

"Action, obviously."

"Obviously," she said, a teasing gleam in her eyes, "*Rogue One* or Jason Bourne?"

"Do you really need to ask? Jason Bourne. All those super-cool operative skills."

The look on her face was dubious at best. "Oh, right, I can definitely see that."

He reached for the edge of the blanket and tugged her closer. "Hey, don't doubt me. I am *all* about the covert…"

"Action?"

"Exactly," he said with a small smile. "The spontaneous covert *action*." He added the word to the Scrabble board, noting that, despite the rain pummeling the island, he felt lighter than he had in years. *Nice to have a woman around.* "And you?" he asked, tilting his head to catch her gaze. "I imagine you love romance."

"Obviously."

"Sweet or sexy?"He held her gaze, noting the way her eyes darkened slightly. Almost as if she…what? Wanted to kiss him as much as he wanted to kiss her? God, he hoped he was that lucky.

She moved the strap of the dress back onto her shoulder, a casual move that sent a shot of unexpected raw desire through his system. "Both."

"Best answer so far." If she wasn't the sweetest, sexiest woman he'd seen in a while…*damn.*

Blame it on the storm, or the unexpected intimacy of the situation, whatever the reason, in that moment, he knew one thing. If this woman gave even the smallest indication that she wanted to kiss him, then *not* kissing her was going to be next to impossible.

"What about your favorite breakfast?"

"Do I like it sweet or sexy?"

"No—I mean, well, sweet, maybe, if you like Belgian waffles or French toast or… "

"Coffee. Just coffee." He nodded toward the Thermos. "But a bagel from Shelsky's on Court Street? Definitely sexy. The sexiest in Brooklyn."

"The sexiest, huh?"

"By far."

She laughed again—and *damn*. He was grinning. "So is Shelsky's, home of the world's sexiest bagel, your *favorite* breakfast place?"

"Not by a long shot," he said, leaning closer, his smile still playing at the edges of his mouth. Because, God help him, she was making him feel more alive than he had in a long time. Another subtly sexy comment or two would show if she was feeling the same way. And he hoped she did. "No, my favorite breakfast place is in bed."

Her lips rounded into a small circle. "Oh…well, that *is* sexy."

"Think it ups the passion threshold?"

"Definitely ups the passion…threshold, yes." She cleared her throat. "Let's move on to the next section. Favorite part about dating."

He leaned closer. "I'd much rather talk about kissing."

Another blush stained her cheeks. "Okay, that's the same area. I guess." She swallowed. "So your favorite part about kissing?"

He'd meant the question to put her on edge, but instead she'd turned it around on him without even trying. "The buildup. The sense that maybe, just maybe, you're going to kiss."

She bit down on her bottom lip as if to hold back her next words. "Me too. I love the good night kiss. The anticipation. The possibilities." She shifted onto her hip and the strap of her dress fell away, leaving only the red lace of her bra against her bare shoulder. His mouth went dry. *So many possibilities.*

She looked over at him. Caught his gaze. Held it. "So…when was the last time you gave someone a good night kiss?"

"Too long," he said in a low voice. "Far too long."

He smiled. She smiled back. "So when is a good night kiss appropriate?" she asked. "After the first date? Or maybe… the second?"

Or now. Right now.

"A better question might be: why limit a kiss to good night?" He leaned closer, his gaze drifting to her mouth. Jesus, he wanted to kiss her. Wanted to find out if her lips tasted like strawberries. He felt certain they would.

"That *is* a much better question."

Her answer was a near whisper, soft and sweet, and he couldn't take his eyes off those soft, crushable lips. He shifted closer, wanting to feel her mouth beneath his, wanting to kiss her until she was gasping for breath. But could he trust those desires? Hell, it'd been forever since he wanted to carry a woman across her passion threshold—any threshold. But with *this* woman…"A kiss is just the beginning."

He looked at Kate. She looked back. They'd both been hurt, and while she still believed in love, love was out of the question for him. But he could be her rebound guy. Make her feel things she'd never felt before. Give her all the hot chips she deserved. "A kiss can lead anywhere."

"Anywhere?" A quiet sigh fell from her parted lips, inviting him closer. "One little kiss?"

"One little kiss." His full attention focused on her mouth. "Never had a kiss lead…anywhere."

He could stop here. Back away before this went any further. Maybe he should. She wanted this and had been plain that she wasn't expecting anything, but he'd been here before. Taken chances. Let his heart—and other things—guide him.

"Are you sure you can still kiss, considering how it's been 'far too long?'"

"Excuse me?"

A mischievous twinkle at the back of her eyes. "You heard me."

"That sounds like a challenge." She wet her lips, a move so enticing that he knew he was going to kiss her if he didn't stop *right now*. "I love a good challenge."

Her eyes grew wide. "Who doesn't?"

A low chuckle sounded in the back of his throat. Damn, this was fun. *She* was fun. He gave the blanket a quick tug, and suddenly, she was just inches way. He slanted his mouth over her already parted lips, hovering there in anticipation, feeling her warm breath. In that moment, he almost believed a kiss could lead anywhere. He brushed her lips gently, barely a touch, and she let go a soft sigh. An invitation.

His lips captured hers again, tenderly, as his hands moved up her back and tangled in the curls at the nape of her neck. He deepened his kiss slowly, adding intensity with her every quiet sound of encouragement. God, he'd missed the feel of a woman in his arms, and this woman made him realize *just* how much he'd been missing. Made him feel how much he wanted her, maybe even needed her, if just for this one night. Here. In the middle of the storm.

He pulled away slowly and took in the sight of her. Eyes gone dark, her lips wet from kissing, her skin flushed and warm—she was the prettiest thing he'd seen in a very long time.

A *very* long time.

"Great kiss."

"*Great* kiss."

He raised his eyes to meet her gaze, not quite believing what he was about to say. "Kate, I may not be that whole company-line package, but I *can* promise you more great kisses, and if you'll let me show you exactly where a kiss can lead…" He stopped. Drew in a breath. *What the hell? Nothing to lose.* "I can guarantee you really great sex."

Chapter Six

Guarantee? Had she heard him right? *Guaranteed great sex.*

Kate felt her racing heart stop. Great sex wasn't something she'd experienced with her ex. Or maybe ever. And here he was — after delivering one heck of a kiss — guaranteeing heart-stoppingly great sex. She wrapped her arms around her body to keep from shivering with anticipation. "That's a pretty big promise."

He smiled as if *big* wasn't a problem, a boyish grin lighting up his face. "Well, hot chips are my specialty, so I'm pretty certain I can deliver."

Her heart rate accelerated, but hey, she enjoyed a challenge as much as the next girl. She'd certainly enjoyed the last one, she thought, drawing in a steadying seven-second breath. "What makes you so sure you can deliver?"

He took off his glasses and looked her in the eye. "It's the way I kiss."

The way I kiss. She drew in another breath. *Wow.* The effect of those eyes without the Costellos was — wow. Butterflies in the stomach. For the first time, the expression made sense.

The way I kiss. Four little words, and all of a sudden, she was melting. "You sure are confident."

He shrugged a broad shoulder. "Really great sex starts with a really great kiss, and maybe it's been a while, but some things you never forget."

"Like riding a bike?"

A wicked smile played at the edge of his mouth. "Nothing like riding a bike, sweetheart."

Sweetheart. Kate had never liked the nickname. Always the sweet one, the considerate one, she felt the expectation of the moniker. But from his lips, the endearment sounded more like an invitation than a demand. And this was an invitation she wanted to accept.

"What do you say, Kate?" His gaze dropped to her mouth. "Interested?"

Her mouth went dry. *Say something.* She cleared her throat. God, yes, she was interested. He fit the bill perfectly. He wasn't super-vain, or pathological, or gorgeous beyond reason. He was scruffy and cute. *Safe.* She bit down on her lower lip. Of course, that last kiss wasn't exactly what she'd call *safe*, but she'd only be here for twenty-four hours—she could keep it simple. She ran her tongue over her lips. *Now or never, Kate.* This was her chance to be a *Cosmo* girl. Live out a few of those fantasies she wrote about.

She shifted her body closer to the game board, picked up three Scrabble letters, and laid down her answer. YES. "One more kiss and we'll see where it leads."

He added three letters to the game for a triple word score.

Y

E

K I S S

One more kiss. Yes, please.

Jake looked up from the board, his blue eyes locked with hers, shadows from the candlelight emphasizing the planes of his face, and suddenly, it felt impossible to swallow.

"Do you know the three elements of the perfect kiss?" he asked.

The timbre of his voice dipped into a low hum that made her toes curl into the luxurious blanket. "No, but I'm sure you do."

He actually had the nerve to look pleased with himself. "I do."

The rush of her feelings was strange and unexpected, and whether she owed her daring to the situation, the intimacy of the candlelight, or the fact that they were alone, safe inside as the storm raged outside, didn't seem to matter. "Plan on sharing?"

"First, don't rush it." He eased his long frame closer, looped his index fingers beneath the straps of her sundress, and tugged gently on the straps.

"Slow and easy." Her voice was a whisper as her gaze fell to his lips.

His mouth tilted closer. "Secondly, it is critical…"

"Critical?" she whispered, her gaze locked on his mouth.

"*Critical.*" The straps fell from her shoulders as his fingertips coasted along the lines of her collarbone. "To minimize distractions."

"Minimize distractions," she repeated. His hands drifted south, grazing the neckline of her dress before moving over her nearly naked shoulders. "I am so not distracted."

A smile lifted the edges of his mouth, and he took her face in his both hands. "Timing is everything."

Wow. There it was again, that *wow, wow, wow* feeling. She felt hypnotized as his lips moved closer, not touching but just a breath away.

Her everyday seemed distant and unreal. *Timing is everything*, he'd said, and Hallelujah, her time was now. He leaned closer, and the way his muscles moved beneath the cotton of his T-shirt made the breath catch in her throat. The storm raged outside, but the candlelit house felt intimate, hushed except the rain against the skylights. Her eyes drifted shut. *Now. Kiss me now.*

And he did. Slowly. Deeply. Indulging in her. Kissing her like it was a kind of mindful meditation.

The moment felt dreamy. Nothing like New York. No taxis or traffic, no takeout guy at the door, no police sirens or ferry horns. Just the circling wind and rain and the two of them together for the night

Not wanting the moment to end, she laced her fingers in the curls at the nape of his neck and pulled him closer. Yes, he was still her interview, but she wanted this night and she didn't want it to end with just one kiss.

Her lips parted, and a soft moan escaped her. The fragrant, vanilla-scented air, the sexy blues on the radio, the fierce warmth of his kiss raced straight to her head. His hands fell to her hips and coaxed her an inch closer, close enough to feel his warm breath against her cheek as he pulled back. His blue eyes darkened with desire, and his gaze seared her flushed skin, promising all kinds of torturous delight.

His gaze dipped to her mouth as though he wanted to kiss her again. Desire kicked in as an image of the two of them rolling around like thunder beneath the soft gray sheets of his California King blossomed in her mind like an island flower. *Bring on the fantasy.* She brought his mouth crashing back down onto hers, twisting her hands into his dark hair, not caring that it curled wildly in all the wrong places, wanting only to stay in his arms and in his kiss. His hands fell to her ass and dragged her closer. Her heart pounded in her chest. His mouth on hers. His hands burning across her skin. New and unfamiliar. And she loved it.

Her body melted into his, and the slim space between them disappeared, their heartbeats pulsing in time with the rhythm of the wind. She pulled him closer, wrapping her elbows around his neck, entwining her fingers deeper into his soft hair, pressing her body closer. She breathed in his scent of spiced rum and ocean air, and pulled him closer, wanting to feel every muscle in his body contract beneath her fingers.

"Are you sure?" he whispered against her lips. "Because if you're not, you need to tell me now."

"I am so sure." She tugged at the bottom of his t-shift, and her hands skimmed the muscles of his abdomen. "Completely, totally off the record sure."

She wanted this feeling. This rush of sensation. Didn't need a plan beyond when she would feel his mouth again.

He pressed another kiss against her mouth. But it wasn't enough, not nearly enough. God, she'd forgotten how it felt to be desired. To be kissed with intention. To be wanted. Heck, maybe she'd never known. Not like this. The new Kate had arrived. "What happens in Paradise…"

• • •

Jake needed no more encouragement.

He brushed a white-blonde curl from her cheek as his lips covered hers, teasing and gentle at first, growing more insistent as he traced the line of her lips with his tongue, stopping at the corners to tug at her bottom lip. He heard her soft intake of breath. *Slow and steady. Critical timing.* All of it. *Out the freaking window.*

And when her lips parted under his kiss, he accepted her enticing invitation and deepened his exploration of her mouth. At the first caress of his tongue inside her mouth, an earthy moan rose from her throat. His heart raced, beating steadily against the gauzy material of her red dress, meager protection against the heat building between them.

His hands moved from her rounded hips, along the gentle

curve of her waist to the swell of her breasts. He tugged the small strap and the fabric fell away, allowing him access to the edges of the lacy bra that had been tempting him for hours. Her head tilted back in an invitation, and his mouth moved to her throat, licking and tasting, enjoying the feel of her, letting his hands roam her breasts. He kneaded the soft flesh, tweaking the pointed tips until she arched forward to fill his hands more completely, reveling in the soft, pleading whimpers falling from her lips.

Damn, it had been too long since he'd had a woman in his arms—way too long—and her sweet, sexy sounds made him want more. So much more. She edged her body closer, silently asking for his touch, and turning back now felt impossible. Instead, he circled the edge of her nipple, first with his palm, then with the tips of his fingers, pinching and tweaking as his tongue licked and kissed through the lace. He nipped at the rosy peaks, loving the way her body trembled, responding to his every bite and touch. *To hell with self-control.* He released a low growl of need as his hands fell to her hips and flipped her onto her stomach.

A soft moan escaped her as his fingers drifted to the hem of her dress. He lowered his body carefully, letting her feel some of his weight, adjusting his position to allow his fingers to slip beneath the thin fabric of the dress. Creating an intimate trail across the curve of her calves, he lifted the dress higher to the reveal the creamy skin of her thighs, then shifted his body higher to kiss the back of her neck. "Is this okay," he asked, his fingers skimming the line of her body. "Is this what you want?"

She turned her head to catch her lips. "Yes," she whispered.

And that word was everything he needed to hear.

He tugged away the small straps of her dress to reveal the naked skin of her shoulders and back, the shapely line of her body. He slipped the cotton away from her skin and his kiss traveled across her back, her ribs, along the delicate lines of her shoulder blades, the back of her neck. She twisted toward him, softly whimpering, wanting more.

But he wasn't finished showing her all the erotic places a kiss might lead.

With one of his knees between her legs, he fell back on his haunches as his hands moved to her hips and slipped under the hem of the dress to burn an intimate trail along the inside of her thighs. He'd never felt so turned on, so invested in showing a woman all the pleasures of her body. What was it about her that made him feel lighter, more free than he'd felt in years? He wanted her to feel free, too. Maybe he couldn't give her everything. But he could give her this.

Easing his body closer, he let his fingers slip inside her panties. She was wet, ready. Her body moved against his playing fingers, eager to find release. His thumb circled, easing in and out of her in time with the seductive thrusts of his hips from behind. His mouth moved against her neck and jaw, tracing a hot, wet line to her earlobe as his hands continued to work her breasts and her clit. She arched back, giving him more access to her body, and for the love of Jesus, he'd never seen a sexier woman in his entire life. But he wasn't done. Not by a long shot.

He pressed her body back down with his and whispered against her ear. "I want to make you come. Now. Right now."

"Yes," she whispered, "Now."

His hands at her hips, he flipped her onto her back. His mouth found her lips, kissing her deeply as he slipped his fingers deeper inside her, sending tiny bolts of lightning flashing through her. "Come for me, Kate."

"Yes," she said, her breathing ragged as she edged closer. "Don't stop. Please don't stop."

Her naked pleading thrilled him to his core. He wanted to give her more. *Oh God, this is definitely not good.*

He knew it as his mouth captured her soft strawberry lips. He knew it when his hands coaxed her to the edge, and her pleading sounds turned to satisfied cries, the pleasure rushing through her body as he guided her through a series of tremors. He knew.

This is better than good.

This is fucking great.

All he cared about was *feeling*. Feeling her body. Feeling her move. Feeling her body come apart with pleasure. Damn, he wanted more of her now. *Right here. Now. In the middle of this storm.* He wanted to make her body thrill while he drove inside her until she begged him to make her come. Again and again and again.

Stuck here all night.

He made a low sound at the back of his throat. The last time his body had craved a woman like this was ages ago. So long ago he couldn't remember. If he'd ever craved a woman so desperately. He wasn't sure. Maybe it was because he'd been in a sex-free zone for longer than he cared to admit. But this woman? He couldn't keep his hands off her. He tugged her close, and together they fell back against the Scrabble board. He shoved it aside. *Guaranteed.* He should stop. *Great sex.*

Her hands moved to the waist band of his low-slung sweats, and with her gaze locked onto his, she slipped her hand inside and pressed her palm against the bulge in his boxer briefs. He groaned, so ready.

Unable to wait, he dragged his sweats and underwear past his hips and kicked them onto the blanket. A smile spread across his face, and he eased her panties over her hips enough to slide his fingers back inside her. She was so slick and wet. So ready. Again. His fingers worked her delicately, bringing her closer and closer to the edge. But this time, he didn't let her come.

He pressed his fingers deep inside and flicked her clit with his thumb, loving the raw need etched across her features, all laid out for him to see. Her body shuddered as his fingers circled her core, easing in and out of her

"Does that feel good?" he asked, his breathing shallow, every part of him waiting for her response. "Do you want more?"

She answered without words, bringing his mouth crashing down on hers, as she tugged his shirt away, her body bucking against his playing fingers, her hips rising and falling in a series of small pleading movements.

Jesus, Jake hadn't thought it was possible to get any harder, but he was wrong. So wrong. His body literally ached with need. "I want to be inside you."

"Yes," she said. "God, yes."

Outside, hurricane winds roared, but the tropical storm was nothing compared to the fever-pitch of desire raging inside him. He slipped her rumpled dress from her body and tossed it aside, leaving her naked except for her lacy red bra. With just the small scrap of lace between them, they lay together, practically naked in the dim light, the sound of the rain falling in a hush around them. His eyes roamed the curves of her candlelit body, taking in the gentle curve of her stomach, the way her nipples hardened with need, and her breath grew shaky as her body trembled with anticipation. He took his time, stroking her everywhere, tormenting every inch of her body, until the ache inside him demanded more.

Every fiber of his body pulsed, aware of every inch of her as he positioned his hips above her. His eyes locked onto hers as he cradled her body against his.

"You are so pretty." Her mouth reached up to catch his in reply. He kept right on kissing her, licking, swirling until she shivered uncontrollably. As he directed her hand inside her panties, he whispered against her throat, "Show me what turns you on."

And with her gaze still locked with his, she dipped her fingers inside her core for him. So erotic. So *intimate*. He stayed. Watched her touch herself. Noticed her skin grow flushed and pink and pretty, and goddamn, she looked so fucking sexy. Her hips rose as small sweet sounds of desire escaped her. When she was close, he dropped a kiss on her mouth, his lips lingering as he whispered, "Be right back. Stay ready for me."

A desperate moan of protest escaped her swollen lips as he rolled away. His long strides covered the space to his bedroom in record time. He grabbed a blue foil packet from his nightstand—his one and only he kept there. If there was going to be another round, they'd have to break into the stash he had in his closet or the bathroom…or somewhere. Hell, he'd find them. He rushed back, hoping to God there'd be more than one round. She was still there, naked except for the lace. The sight of her pleasuring herself, keeping her body ready to accept his, turned him on in a way he could not explain.

He lowered his body next to her, and she reached for him, rolling the condom over his aching cock, her light touch making him desperate. His mouth fell to hers, and he pulled her close, their heated bodies searching for each other. When they could wait no longer, he entered her slowly, allowing her to accept him, increasing his rhythm as her hips moved upward, her rising body welcoming him deep inside. But it wasn't enough. Not nearly enough. He wanted to her hear cry out his name. Wanted to feel her come apart while his cock was inside her.

He moved deeper, stroking her delicate insides, searching for that sweet spot, pushing her to the limits of pleasure.

"Come for me again, Kate," he whispered against her lips. Her breathing grew ragged, and she bit down hard on her bottom lip, whimpering softly, desperately close to climax. He drove deeper, aiming for the place he knew would make her shatter. A pleading sound erupted from her throat as he guided her through a series of a small earthquakes coaxing her to orgasm once on her own, before enticing another climax to match his. As the candles flickered all around them, she curled against his naked, spent body in a way that spelled out more than a one-night stand of guaranteed great sex.

Damn, he thought, kissing the edge of her temple in a gesture so sweet and romantic, it literally surprised him. YES. The word echoed through his brain, a small word loaded with meaning, a small word that could change everything. He drew in a long breath and pulled her close. YES. Outside, the driving rain continued, and they lay together on the cozy blanket, listening in the dark as the wind swirled and howled like some kind of out-of-control promise. But he wasn't a man who believed in promises. Or soul mates. He was a man who was finished with love.

Tomorrow she'd go back to the city. And he'd stay here. But right now, tonight, he wanted this woman. He wanted her in any and every way she'd take him. His fingers trailed along the curve of her naked hip, and she glanced up at him, a sexy smile lifting the edges her lips. *Great sex, guaranteed.*

Too bad it all ended tomorrow.

Chapter Seven

Wow. So…that happened.

How it'd happened, she wasn't 100 percent sure. Well, she was… A game of Scrabble, a guarantee, the perfect kiss…but still. *Wow.*

So where was her oh-so-willing-to-please bachelor? She blinked her now familiar surroundings into focus: the dark gray walls, the high thread count sheets that would have cost her a week's salary, the yummy, nearly naked man stepping into the room from the shower.

Double wow.

Jake gave her a half-smile. "Morning."

A sigh escaped her. Literally escaped her; she couldn't have prevented it if she'd tried.

Conjuring up a been-here-before smile, she rolled onto her left hip and struck her best *Cosmo* girl pose. "Good morning to you, too."

He responded to her obvious flirtation by anchoring the towel at his waist. She bit down on her bottom lip. Last night with Jake had been phenomenal. She hadn't known two people could generate that kind of heat. In her past relationships, she hadn't felt a fraction of the raw desire or slow satisfaction that had flooded her system with him. And looking at him now, in all his half-naked glory, she was ready to do it again.

Shockingly ready.

Kate watched as he strolled over to the dresser, opened a drawer, and pulled out a pair of faded Levis and a gray T-shirt. Her gaze zeroed in on the jeans. Denim was definitely not conducive to an encore. Hoping he'd take a hint, she let the sheet drop a lower, revealing a little cleavage. But instead of forgoing the clothes, he yanked the towel away, tossed it playfully in her direction, and stepped into the jeans. Commando-style. She liked it. Of course, she'd like it better if he climbed back into bed.

Instead, he walked over and dropped a quick kiss on her mouth. "Do you want coffee?"

She blinked. Could he really be talking about coffee? Because all she could think about was how to get him to unzip his jeans. "Yes," she said. "Coffee's good."

"Okay, then. I'll get the caffeine rolling." He yanked the shirt over his head — more's the pity — and picked up his glasses from the nightstand and settled them against the bridge of his nose. "I need to make a few repairs, but I promise I'll be done in time to take you to the airport in time for your flight."

All her dreamy notions about romantic afternoons and more mind-blowing sex careened to a sudden halt. "My flight?"

"Back to Manhattan. The charters will be running again by this afternoon."

She heard him talking, but she failed to comprehend. Yes, it'd been one night, but…he'd already booked her flight? The one-two combo of anger and disappointment jabbed at her insides, an emotional sequence too complicated to contemplate, so she shoved it aside. "You booked my flight?"

"I reviewed the schedule, made sure flights were taking off." He took a step back. *Physical distance, check. Emotional distance, double-check.* His ex must've really done a number on him. "But I can book it, if you'd like."

"No, I can take care of it." *One night. No interview.* A man of his word. Despite all her cool girl thoughts, she'd not been ready.

He rubbed a hand across the heavy stubble on his jaw. Buried his hands in his pockets. Cleared his throat. "Okay, then."

"Okay," Kate said, forcing an ease into her voice she didn't feel. She tugged the sheet up an inch or two. They'd been clear that this was a one-night stand. But she couldn't shake the feeling that she wanted something more. A two-night stand. A three-night stand. A...

A what? A relationship?

No. She was here to try out not rushing headlong into that self-defeating goal.

Jake gestured toward the bathroom. "You know where everything is...towels and..." His words trailed off as his gaze fell on the red bra peeking out from beneath the sheet. He cleared his throat again. A habit she suddenly found annoying. "Take your time."

She wrapped the sheet around her backside and tugged the scrap of lacy material back under the sheet with her toes. "Thank you."

"Of course." He bent to brush another swift kiss across her mouth, shoved his hands back into his pockets, and wandered out of the room.

She watched him go, her body aching in all the right places, his musky male scent still clinging to her skin. Her mouth twisted to one side. Clearly, she'd been wrong about one thing. Great sex was *not* necessarily part of the whole star-spangled, bells ringing, love-forever package. Not always.

Because no matter how incredible she'd felt last night, no matter how great the sex, Jake Wright was obviously not The One.

For starters, he lived in a cliffside stronghold where he probably never heard more than the wind. She lived in a city with subway grime and commuter noise, where every corner housed a Starbucks ready to pony up a Venti Bold Pick of the Day. He wanted to hide. She wanted to *live*. To grab the Big Apple by its stem and take a big bite out of it. She wanted to be so much more than that pretty girl from Ohio. She wanted to be out there, feeling the pulse of the world.

More than anything, she wanted to love. Real love. Deep down and forever. Jake Wright may have written all those beautiful words in his book, but obviously, great sex aside, he was a man who refused to believe in relationships. Heck, he was maybe incapable of offering one anymore. And for better or worse, she was a girl looking expectedly for love.

But did that really have to be a deal breaker?

True, the fact he'd practically booked her flight home stung, but she'd enjoyed last night—more than she imagined possible. Chasing *love* had only brought her lousy dates and heartache. Instead of worrying about finding the right guy and the right relationship, she should be focusing on having fun, on enjoying her life.

Commit to *not* looking.

Maybe that was what Deepak Chopra meant by the Law of Least Effort. If she stopped looking for that perfect man, stopped expending all her effort trying to create the *right* kind of romantic relationship, and instead, focused on living her life, then The One would find *her*.

No more planning relationships. *Yes. Absolutely.* But that didn't mean she couldn't plan other things, things like an interview with a reluctant bachelor. She eyed a teeny-tiny bikini peeking from the top of her bag, a *new* plan developing in her brain,

One night. No interview—fine. But the night was officially over.

He wanted to book her flight. No more guaranteed great sex? Fine. No more *guarantees* at all, she thought, pulling the bikini from her bag. Last night may have been off the record, but this morning? Well, she was for damn sure not leaving without her interview.

Kate tossed aside the sheet and climbed out of bed. Mr. Ex–Sex Factor had better get ready, because this love blogger still had a few cards to play, and more than a few questions for her bachelor. A small smile touched her lips. Like it or not, *today* was totally on the record.

. . .

While he waited for Kate, Jake busied himself with the removal of the hurricane panels. Anything to keep from striding inside, slipping into the shower, and pressing her slick, naked body up against the cool tile. *Dammit—no.* Where was his famous self-control? A ten second shower fantasy had his dick twitching in his pants.

Sure, he'd enjoyed last night. What red-blooded male wouldn't have? The heat between them had been unbelievable, a fact he'd simply chalked up to his non-existent sex life. But now, he wanted more.

Waking up next to her this morning, listening to her soft breathing, seeing her so cozy and vulnerable, he'd felt… hell, he didn't know what he felt, but he didn't want to feel anything. Not cozy. Not vulnerable. *Nothing.* Not even the fact that he wanted to bury himself inside her more than… *Jesus Christ—no.* He slammed the hammer hard against the side of the panel. *No.*

Needing distraction this morning, he'd called the resort

to check on the safety of the guests, verify the restoration of power, authorize clean-up crews. He'd accomplished a lot while Goldilocks slept. Even managed to confirm the availability of her flight back to Manhattan. Made him feel like a real asshole later, watching her try to cover her disappointment.

The muscles in his jaw tensed. Hurting her had not been his intention. He was a fixer, not a man who broke hearts into uneven pieces.

This was why he didn't date anymore, including what they'd done last night.

But revising his "one night, no interview" commitment wasn't an option. Kate Bell needed to head back to the city, and he needed to keep his freaking wits about him. Before he did something stupid. Like ask her ask to let him explore every delicious inch of her depths. Listen to her honeyed sounds. Make her crazy. Blow. Her. Mind. He felt his throat constrict. Hadn't thought of that one for a while. Hadn't wanted to.

After trading the hammer for a power drill, he set the bit against the plywood and started into the panel. But when Kate sashayed onto the wraparound porch, Jake took one look at her, forgot to release the go button on the drill, and drove a hole straight through the storm cover.

"*Dammit.*"

He yanked the tool away. So much for his custom-made shutters.

Fighting back a smile, she eyed his drill bit. "Need help?"

"No, I do not need…" *Aw, fuck.*

Jake pointed the tool toward the ceiling and tried to breathe. He needed oxygen. Why was no oxygen going to his brain? Maybe because most of the oxygenated blood in his body was rushing due south. Then again, how could he blame his brain for allowing the detour?

The deep-coral bikini top she wore hugged her curves,

dipping low enough in front to give him a delicious glimpse of cleavage. The itsy bitsy bottom, and about a mile and a half of silky smooth legs, were wrapped up in a gauzy skirt tied lazily at the curve of her hip. As she moved toward him, the skirt fell away to expose a flash of creamy thigh and he envisioned those legs wrapped around his waist. Man, she looked even sexier now than she'd looked an hour ago, naked, tucked underneath his sheets.

"Nice bikini," he said, amazed to have strung two words together.

"Thank you." Kate smoothed her skirt over the curve of her hip, and his mouth went dry. Seemingly unaware of the effect of the simple gesture, she stepped closer and eased the drill from his hand. "Maybe you better let me take over from here."

His male ego kicked in. "I can finish."

"Oh, I know," she said, letting the whirr of the drill bit add punch to her words. "But I'd like to offer you a deal." Her mile-long legs climbed up the aluminum step ladder, and the sway of her ass sent his brain along another detour. He tried to focus on her deal. "For every hurricane panel I remove in under forty seconds, you answer one interview question."

"And if you fail?"

A smile lifted the edges of her mouth as if failure was impossible. "I'll tell Jane her match was a miss. No more interview. No more bachelor."

He crossed his arms over his chest. "Ever."

"Ever?"

"That's right. She drops the subject entirely."

"Jake…I can't guarantee she won't try again."

He raised an eyebrow. "You're very convincing. I'm sure you can make it happen."

She pursed her lips, like she was considering every possibility. "This'll either be the shortest interview in the history of interviews, or…"

"Or you get exactly what you want." Jake looked at her. No doubt about it, she held a tool like a pro, but the kind of speed she'd promised required top-notch execution. No way could she do it. He grinned. Ten minutes, he'd be an interview-free zone. "I'll take that deal."

Her ensuing smile was sugar-sweet and innocent, but the gleam in the back of those mischievous green eyes sent a different message: *game on, sucker.*

She tossed him her phone with the stopwatch app open on the screen, and in less than six minutes, she'd removed all the panels protecting the windows of the wraparound porch, stacked them by the door, and handed him the drill. *So much for less-than-superior execution.* The woman could probably operate a high-speed power tool in her sleep.

Jesus Christ.

He shot her a sidelong glance. "Guess I owe you a few answers."

"Six, to be precise." She nodded toward the windows lining the back of the house. "Unless you want to go for more."

He stabbed at his glasses and handed her the phone. "Better quit while I'm ahead."

He'd answer her six questions. After all, she'd won fair and square, and he was a fair and square kind of guy. But if they were going to spend the afternoon trading more of her sexy questions, keeping his hands to himself might prove to be impossible. *Especially given the way she looks in a bikini.* Time to conjure up that famous self-control of his.

Her flight back to New York was confirmed.

For better or worse, he wasn't about to change his mind about relationships. Still a matchmaking-free zone. She was a Relationship girl. Seeing her try to cover her feelings earlier? He wasn't going to hurt her again.

Truth be told, he wasn't that mad about having to do the

interview. At least this would help her career. He couldn't offer her anything beyond last night, but at least he could offer her this. First things first, though. They had to get out of here. If he was going to do an interview, it would be as far away from anyone else as possible.

He tucked a flyaway hair behind her ear. "We can't do the interview here. Ready to take a ride?"

Her answering smile was slow and knowing. Like last night's sex. He shrugged. *Well, it was a good question. A very good question.* He pointed toward his vintage Ducati. "*That* is our ride."

On impulse, he'd parked there earlier. He loved that bike. He'd relinquished most of his former high-flying lifestyle, but the motorcycle? The motorcycle he'd kept.

Kate eyed the bike with a healthy mix of suspicion and fear. "You're joking, right?"

"Aw, c'mon now, Miss Frequent Flyer." He reached past her and lifted his leather bomber from an outside hook near the door. "Afraid of racing down the open road with me?"

Her expression said it all. *Yes. Hell, yes.*

He wrapped the jacket over her shoulders and pulled her close. "Bikini and leather. Not motorcycle club approved," he said, resisting the urge to place a fast kiss on her mouth. "Looks good on you, though." He linked his fingers through hers and led her across the fifty yards to his workshop. "C'mon, you need a helmet and, while I hate to lose the view" — he gave her bare legs a lazy glance — "a pair of jeans, too."

Her eyes narrowed. "Which you just happen to have."

He tossed out a teasing, not-so-boyish grin, "Always prepared."

The sound she made in response spoke volumes about how she felt about *that.*

He chuckled, punched the code into the keypad, and waited as the workshop door rumbled open. Inside, he opened the closet and grabbed a pink motorcycle helmet and a pair of very feminine, very sexy dark denim jeans.

"These ought to work," he said, turning to Kate.

Her gaze was glued to the jeans, her expression now telegraphing a seven word question: *who the hell do those belong to?* He grinned again. His love blogger was jealous, and he'd be damned if that idea didn't please the hell out of him.

He winked. "I'm pretty certain my sister packed that pink duffle bag, and since she failed to pack you a pair of jeans, you can borrow hers." He pressed the jeans into her hands.

"How did you know?" She stopped. Shook her head. "Doesn't matter." Making little circles in the air with her index finger, she looked over at him, the expression on her face as prim and proper as her bikini would allow. "Turn around."

Jake couldn't help a small chuckle. "I've already seen what's underneath that bikini." He set the helmet on the table and took a step closer. "In fact, I've already *enjoyed* what's underneath that bikini."

He reached for the edge of her wrap, and she backed up another step, pressing her gorgeous backside against his Chris Craft cruiser. What he wouldn't give to coax her out of her bikini and into that boat for an afternoon of lovemaking. But—no.

He brushed a strand of hair away from her cheek and bent his head to breathe in the cherry blossom scent of her skin. *Damn.* Not a good idea. Her scent reminded of springtime in New York. Keeping control of himself wasn't going to be easy.

She turned her face toward his, her lips parted, her breathing soft and sweet—

And yep, willpower was a finite resource, because this time he couldn't help but kiss her, his lips falling to hers as if drawn in by some gravitational force. He kissed her slowly, pressing her body up against the smooth planks of the boat as she returned the kiss, sinking her fingers into his hair to pull him closer.

He took pleasure in the kiss, the press of her lips against his, the feel of this woman in his arms. He ran his hands down her waist, settled on her hip and slowly ended the kiss, letting his mouth linger against her lips. She looked up at him, flushed and beautiful. He felt unsettled, off-balance somehow. This woman arrived on his island and shot his peace all to hell in ways he didn't dare contemplate. He took a small step back, his hands falling from her hips.

"If you want to see the rest of this island, you better get those jeans on so we can ride. Now." *Right now.* Before they wound up creating more trouble than he'd bargained for.

After a moment's hesitation, she slipped around the hull, presumably to untie her silky skirt, wriggle her hips into those sexy jeans.

Self-control, self-control, self-control.

Jake strode across the room. *Distance. Distance is good.* He pulled an old quilt from the closet and grabbed a small bottle of champagne—compliments of one of the resort's vendors—from the workshop fridge. As he closed the door, Kate came back around the boat, and he caught a glimpse of her reflected in the stainless steel. She'd woven the airy skirt through the loops of the jeans like a belt, allowing the floral fabric to float over her hips and thighs. Standing next to *Island Time,* her blonde hair falling across bare shoulders, no makeup or artifice, she looked like some kind of bohemian goddess. She was *beautiful.*

Jake felt something shift inside him. Yesterday he'd expected a hot-shot Manhattan girl, all tailored clothing and New York attitude. But today he was seeing a woman who was soft and lovely and totally unexpected. If he were a better man, the kind capable of feeling and offering the love she needed, he'd be a fool not to try. He just hoped one day she found that man.

He walked over, traded the quilt and champagne for the butterfly-embossed helmet, and settled it squarely on her head. The damn thing made her look even more beautiful.

"Perfect." He choked back his feelings and secured the strap. "Now you look like a biker."

Her dubious look made him smile, and he took her hand and led her outside to the Ducati.

"Are you sure about this?" she asked, eyeballing the bike, pulling the helmet strap tight.

"Yes, I'm sure." While she got used to the idea, he opened the seat trunk, added the champagne to the soft-pack cooler he'd filled this morning while Goldilocks had been sleeping in his bed, and strapped it carefully on the back of the bike.

Kate gazed longingly back at the truck. "Can't we take the Ford?"

"Not as much fun as the bike, sweetheart." He reached into the inside pocket of his leather jacket and traded his specs for a pair of prescription sunglasses. "Trust me," he said in a teasing whisper, "you're going to love it." He straddled the bike and reached out his hand.

She made a defeated sound in the back of her throat, put her hand in his, and climbed onto the back of the bike. With her settled behind him, Jake fired up the bike and accelerated forward. An exhilarated cry escaped her as the coastline disappeared in a rush behind them. When he'd suggested taking the bike to a better place for the interview, he'd stupidly failed to imagine the way she'd look wearing her bikini under his leather jacket or the way she'd feel pressed against him as they zipped along the island roads, outracing the balmy air. Her palms fell low across his abdomen as the twin engines thrummed beneath them. Not exactly a recipe for emotional distance.

"You okay back there?"

He felt her nod against his shoulder blade. "Just stay on the right side of the road."

Without bothering to fight the smile easing across his face, Jake turned the bike onto the narrow road that led to the island's interior. She curled into his back on the curve, and he took pleasure in the feeling of her arms wrapped around him. The way her body tucked into his as he maneuvered the bike. The way her hipbone felt pressed up against his backside.

"Don't worry," he called back into the wind, "you're safe with me."

But was *he*? Last night had been incredible, and yes, okay, probably just a function of being alone for so long, and yet, part of him wanted her to stay.

He shifted down to release the clutch and brought the motorcycle to a stop along the edge of a hidden cove on the far side of the island. His favorite place. He hadn't planned on coming here, but…"Welcome to Memory Cove." He accepted the helmet she handed him and tried not to think too much about why he brought her here. To this place. "Caribbean legend says the memories of a day spent here can't be forgotten."

"Pretty romantic." Sitting astride the bike, she shrugged his jacket away from her shoulders like some kind of island fantasy come to life. "Any memories you can't forget?"

He hung the helmet on the handlebar, pretty certain he'd never forget this woman straddling his bike, slipping out of his leather bomber, challenging his solitude. "On the record?"

"On the record." A smile moved slowly across her pretty face, an inviting smile that called to the impulsive desires simmering beneath his skin.

"No memories," he said with a shake of his head. "Not yet, anyway."

She peeked over at him. "Maybe we can change that."

His gaze gravitated to the exposed curve of her neck. The

damned strings on her bikini practically whispered, "Untie me." His slow smile met hers. "Maybe we can."

Careful, Jake. He needed to tamp down his not-to-be-trusted instincts. He twisted a blonde curl around his index finger. This woman had managed to slip under his reserve, chip away at his practiced loneliness. She should have been out on the first flight, but the truth was that he wanted her as badly as he could remember wanting any woman, a literal physical ache. She'd reawakened a combination of sensual and emotional instincts he'd buried a long time ago. Instincts that had brought him pain once before. As he unhooked the cooler from the back of the bike and tucked the faded quilt under his arm, a small part of him worried he'd be less content with his peace after she was gone.

Not that it changes anything, he thought, helping her from the bike. With his fingers linked through hers, he led the way through the natural stone arch, down a hidden staircase lined with sea grapes ripening on vines bent by the storm's wind. He moved at her pace, careful not to rush.

At the bottom, the steps gave way to a quiet beach of white powdery sand and an endless expanse of turquoise blue water. The storm had washed away the island's imperfections, and now the sun shone bright in a cloudless sky, the summer air warm and still. He breathed in, enjoying the way the warm, salty air mixed with the sweetness of the flowers, the sea grapes, the tumbling vines. He still remembered his arrival on the island—a semi-famous guy whose life had turned on him, a neglected city kid trying to outrun his mistakes. The moment his toes sank into the warm sand, he'd felt quiet in his soul. No cameras. No interviews. No runaway celebrity scandal. Just miles of endless blue sky. About as far from Brooklyn as a guy could get. He'd loved it here. He still did.

Inside the cove, red and purple flags flew over an abandoned lifeguard station, indicating high surf level. He'd set them up yesterday before she'd crashed into his peace. He'd take them down later, but for now, the colorful warning afforded some much-desired privacy.

He stole a glance at the woman standing next to him, listened to her breathe in time with the rhythm of the crashing waves, took in the way the tropical bikini top hugged her curves, the way the tight denim jeans coasted past slim ankles to bare feet.

Seclusion never looked better.

Chapter Eight

The shining sun illuminated the white sand of the hidden cove, but she refused to let the romance of the setting distract her from the fact that they were back on the record. Naturally, her heart wanted to indulge in the dream of love after a night of amazing sex, but looking for forever in every man and every relationship never worked. Besides, last night wasn't a relationship. It was a time out from her everyday world. *A wicked, sexy time out.*

Today, she had a new outlook and six questions. Not much, but combined with the allure of a stormy night, his expert status, and a perfect kiss, enough to build an article on. If only he'd be a little more forthcoming.

"I'm waiting on an answer," she said.

"That can't be a real question."

"Does it matter? A deal is a deal, and this is the kind of stuff Smart Cupid readers want to know."

He shook his head. "Listen, just because you conned me into answering a few overly personal questions—"

"I did not con you."

"Are you kidding?" He snapped open the threadbare quilt from the workshop and spread it across the sand. "The shutters, the power tool, the *bikini*?" A hard chuckle erupted from his throat. "I'm a gambler's kid. I know a con job when I see one." She opened her mouth to speak, but he held up his palm. "Six questions—fine. Six answers—no problem. But you want me to share my private, sexual fantasies with a group of readers looking for a Man Candy Crush?" He gave her a look that said something along the lines of, *tough shit on that,* and moved the cooler on to the quilt. "No way. No way in hell."

"Oh, don't take it all so seriously." Kate fought back a self-satisfied smile, less inclined to share him with the women of Manhattan than she'd like to admit. "A crush can be fun."

"Don't get me wrong, I'm enjoying my island candy crush, but if you expect me to sign on Smart Cupid's contractual dotted line so you can splash my bachelor status all over the Internet—yeah, not going to happen."

She held up her hands like she was holding a pen and piece of paper, and she pretended to write. "Note number one: Jake reveals that contrary to popular belief, he will absolutely welch on a bet."

"What? I'm not welching on anything."

She smiled. "Answer. The. Question."

He pulled her close, teasing her—goddamn him—making her as uneasy as she'd made him feel. "If you really want to know," he said in a deeply mischievous tone, "blonde, sweet, sexy as hell…now that's a fantasy I can get behind."

"That is definitely not a legitimate response." She pushed playfully at his shoulders, and he let her go. "We'll come back to that one." She settled primly onto the edge of the faded quilt. "Next question," she continued, all breezy and cool, as if she didn't have a personal interest. "What is the one thing that turns you on most about a woman?"

He chuckled and lowered his body next to hers with an easy grace. "Like I'm going to fall for that one." She opened her mouth to object, but he held up his palm. "I agreed to answer a few questions, not stroll through a minefield of gotcha questions."

"Fine." She pulled a snack-sized bag of chips from the open cooler and hurled it at him. "Let's keep it simple. If you could be anywhere in the world, where would you be?"

"Right here." He tore open the bag and offered it to her. She accepted, nodding her thanks. "I love this place. As kids—me, Janey, Nick—we dreamed about this kind of refuge. Nights my brother waited up for our dad to stumble home, I'd sneak into the attic with my sister and we'd talk about just taking off one day, leaving Brooklyn in the dust."

She grew quiet, surprised both by the way his tone shifted from teasing to reflective, as well as how much he felt comfortable revealing. "Where was your mom?"

"Working two jobs. Every day, every night." He glanced down at the faded quilt, and it struck her that the blanket was probably a Brooklyn castoff. "Trying to fix it. Keep it together."

Kate nodded, understanding. "Must've been tough. Not knowing who to count on."

"We managed." He reached back and pulled a few Tupperware containers from the basket, his tone indifferent, as if he'd revealed nothing. "But a place like Paradise…this was a dream." Picnic arranged, he lifted his wallet from the basket and pulled out a photo he'd had tucked behind his driver's license. "My favorite."

She peeked over at the fading image. "Oh my gosh, Brighton Beach. Is that…"

A quick nod of confirmation and he continued. "Me and Jane, about six and seven, each of us missing a couple of teeth. Nick's on the far right." A fond expression formed on his face as he looked at the picture, three kids, shovels in hand, fake palms behind them bent in the summer breeze. "We spent most summer afternoons skipping stones in the gutter along the East River, shooting off bottle rockets, stupid stuff." He slipped the photo back into his wallet. "But that day, my dad stayed home instead of racing out to bet money we didn't have on the ponies, or drink too much at the Italian-American Club." His jaw visibly tightened. "That day, he drove us from Brooklyn all the way to Brighton. Bought us ice cream, Nathan's hot dogs. Money for the arcade. Let us beat him at Skeeball. A kid's dream."

She gave him what she hoped was an optimistic smile. "That's a nice memory."

Jake tossed the wallet into the basket. "Yeah, well, he took off a few months later."

Her hand fell to his knee. "I'm sorry."

He looked over at her, his expression shuttered, acceptance rather than pain etched into his features. "I think I'd been dreaming of a place like this ever since."

"And when your marriage fell apart…"

"After I figured out I couldn't fix it. I came here—to paradise."

She tilted her head toward the wallet. "But you miss home, your family."

"I do." Without looking at her, he pulled a plastic cup and the small bottle of champagne from the basket. The shift in his tone left little doubt that he'd revealed more than he'd planned. "Home is home, right? For better or worse."

"Home is home." She nodded, searching for a way back to their more intimate conversation. She wanted to know him, not only for the profile, or because she'd won six answers to six questions, but because when she'd read the words in his book, she'd known he was a man capable of real love. She wanted to know that man—even if she wasn't meant to be the one he loved. An unexpected pain stabbed at her insides. Her voice grew quiet. "Do you ever think about writing again?"

"Sometimes." He gave her a guarded look. "When I started out after grad school, I was looking for a job, any job. Ended up loading trucks for UPS at night. That left my days free, so I started writing and then...*The Sex Factor* just took off." His hand cruised through the air at an angle like a jetliner. "But it was never about the bestseller list for me." His mouth twisted to one side. "I really wanted to make a difference in peoples' lives."

He popped the cork and poured the golden liquid into her cup. "I think I was writing about what I thought relationships could be...or should be. Not that I'd experienced it. Then I met my ex and signed on for the celebrity-style life I didn't want..." He let the words fade away, a resigned expression on his face. "Most of the book seems like fantasy stuff now. Rules to romance by." He shook his head.

"Nothing wrong with abiding by the rules," she said, searching for the correct words. "Finding...the right person can be...exhausting." She threw out a bemused smile. "Nothing wrong with having a romantic roadmap. I love your rules. Not that I'm an expert in relationships. Obviously. Considering my string of dating nightmares."

"Which ones do you like?"

"Which dating nightmare?"

He cracked a smile. "Which *rule*?"

"Oh," she said, feeling a blush sting her cheeks. "Pillow talk. Learning what inspires someone."

"Someone?"

"A *man*." She glanced over at him a moment, and felt the now-familiar crackle of electricity between them. "Learning what makes a man want to know a woman...really know her. What makes him want to stay in bed with her and reveal his secrets. What turns him on?" She peered up at him. "What turns *you* on?"

He growled, like the answer wasn't something he wanted to admit. "You know what turns me on."

"Do I?"

"Keep looking at me like that and you'll find out."

She took in his stubbled chin, dark hair in need of a serious cut, those ocean blue eyes. "Tell me."

Her gaze dropped to his lips, and he moved closer, his mouth brushing the edge of her jaw, the touch so brief it might have been her imagination, if not for the sigh that escaped her.

Easing back, he slipped the thin strap of her bikini top over her shoulder. "This turns me on." His palms ran along the collarbone to the side swells of her breasts, and she shivered, despite the warm sun.

"And this." He moved aside the filmy material of her bikini and drank in the sight of her naked skin. "The sight of you. The feel of you." His thumbs grazing her nipples, circling, tweaking, until the tips grew taut and aching with need. "The taste of your skin." He took her nipple into his mouth and sucked on her flesh until she practically whimpered, a soft desperate cry she couldn't hold back. "That's right, all your sexy pleading." He yanked away the remaining material of her bikini top and took her other breast in his mouth, seemingly on a mission to drive her crazy. Another moan escaped her lips. "God, yes, that turns me on." His lips on her warm skin felt so good, so incredibly right. But it wasn't enough. She wanted more.

"*You* turn me on," he whispered, low and rough and with barely-concealed need. His gaze locked onto hers. "Every gorgeous, beautiful inch of you."

His lips bent to lick at her neck, her breasts, down her stomach, across her hip. He was setting her ablaze, bringing out feelings in her she'd never had. Never realized were possible.

You can't plan passion.

Now she knew how true those words were.

God, yes. She wanted more than a simple lesson in what turned him on. She wanted it all, the complete island fantasy — one last sensual experience with this man who made her feel utterly and completely desired. Like an erotic daydream, her time with him was unlocking sensual fantasies she never even knew she had. His hands moved back to the zipper of her jeans. A shiver of excitement coursed through her body as he tugged the denim over her hips and thighs, kissing her inner thigh, behind her knees, her ankles as he worked the fabric away from her body.

He looked up at her, a smile at the edge of his lips. "Know my real sexual fantasy?"

Unable to speak, she shook her head.

"Sex on the beach." He untied one side of her bikini bottom as she'd imagined he would — in one swift tug. "In this deserted cove. With you." He pulled away the second tie, tearing at the fabric. The sound sent a naughty ripple of excitement through her body. "Right now."

Naked beneath his gaze, her breasts swollen, their wet tips aching, her nipples beaded into tight, sensitive knots despite the warm sun, she felt the slick wetness at her core. Trembling with excitement, her hands moved to the waistband of his shirt, but he caught them and pinned them to the side, and pressed her back against the blanket. Heat flooded her body as his mouth drifted south, across her belly, dipping further into her core, the flick of his tongue against her clit setting her on fire.

A desperate whimper hitched in the back of her throat as he moved his mouth away and buried his fingers inside her, demanding the release her body was so ready to give. Shivering as the tantalizing sensations ran through her, her body grew impatient, and she ached to have him fill her. After breaking free, her hands tore open the button of his shorts and tugged them over his hips. He reached back to slip a condom from his pocket and smiled as he tore at the wrapper. "Always prepared." She smiled. "I love that about you."

Together, they struggled to get it on, managing to ramp up one another's need in the process, and when his hands coaxed her body closer, driving his erection down as she rose up to meet him, she cried out in pleasure. She wanted him to remember her like this, reaching for him, taking his body into her, fulfilling his personal fantasy. Her hands curled into the muscles of his broad shoulders. "God, you feel so good. So incredibly...*good*."

His body responded to the obvious need in her voice, driving harder, faster, sinking deeper inside her. She bucked against him, her legs wrapped around his waist, drawing him deeper inside her. Nails digging into his back, she threw her head back, crying out as pleasure crashed through her body as hard as the waves in the distance. She felt the tension ramp up inside his body. Felt his need as he thrust forward, his body shaking, his fingers curled into her hair, his gaze locked onto her face. Moments later, he followed her over the edge, and with the city hundreds of miles away, there was nowhere else in the world she would rather be. Nowhere. "One hell of a fantasy."

His fingers skimmed her hip as she gazed up at him. "One *hell* of a fantasy."

• • •

An hour later, as they wandered by the water, the summer sun shimmering on the waves, the sand beneath his feet, this beautiful woman by his side, Jake felt a knot in his chest.

Having bested the matchmaking attempts of a certain Cupid, they'd soon be back to living their separate lives. He'd continue the renovation of the bungalow. She'd end up with a new and different bachelor. *A different bachelor.* The knot in his chest tightened.

Different time zones. Different lives.

Different *worlds*.

Next to him, Kate leaned over to pick up a sand dollar, rewarding him with a deluxe view of her curves. Man, he really liked her curves, but there was more... She made him *feel*. He swallowed hard. He'd been alone for so long. Did his self-isolation account for the ache in his chest? Or was there more to it?

Not wanting to think, he closed the short distance between, wrapped an arm around her waist, and pulled her swiftly into the surf, beyond the breaking waves, until they were surrounded by the ocean and the quiet. Beneath the cool water, he slipped his thigh between hers, their hips angled but close. Then, in one fluid motion, his lips captured hers. Tenderly at first, his kiss seemed to search for its limits, equal parts poignant and sweet, made more so by the nearness of her departure. His hands moved up her back and tangled in the blonde curls at the nape of her neck.

He knew her rhythms, light and tender, slow and soft, but this felt different. Now, he felt good-bye in her kiss. *Good-bye.*

An unexpected twinge centered in his chest. For a therapist, he fell short on the self-awareness scale, and rather than analyze the pain, he deepened his kiss, anything to avoid thinking about the feeling in his gut that was trying to warn him, screaming at him to get her out of this secluded cove and off the island before he decided he wanted more of her.

More of her.

He kept kissing her, knowing the idea was crazy. There was no way he could wish for more of this woman—any woman—but especially one who valued Relationships with a capitol R. Adorable, sexy women searching for The One were particularly off-limits. He was *not* a Relationship guy. Despite having no role model, he'd wanted a relationship, so he tried. Tried and failed.

But he'd been a damn good therapist. Noticed when people hid their true natures, closed off their desires and emotions. He'd done a helluva lot of closing down himself. But so what? Keeping his emotional distance, not wishing for more, meant never having to face that kind of pain again, and while Kate seemed sweet, he could never risk that kind of agony, that kind of *disappointment* ever again. He wasn't interested in more. But if that was true, why did he hate the thought of her leaving?

Hours ago, she'd arrived on the island, and the sight of her had set off alarm bells. Then she'd barreled into him, and he'd felt the electricity shoot through him like a lightning storm. A summer storm that had set his body on fire. He drew away slowly, and his gaze fell deeper into the eyes of the woman who'd swept onto his island like a force of nature, all wrapped up in a soft, swaying package.

He drew in a breath. No. *No*

He'd simply been charmed by her sweet, cherry-blossom ideas about love—about finding The One. Let her keep her romantic notions. He was the expert who knew better.

Framing her face with his hands, he kissed her one last time, letting his lips linger, taking in her expression, her softly parted lips, her flushed skin.

Her voice was steady and soft. "This is good-bye, then."

A small smile passed over his lips. "Still the ride back to the house." That damn burning sensation extended from his gut to the center of his chest. "I'll take you to the airfield, too. Buy you a martini."

Her fingers entwined with his. "No more martinis. I made it here. I'll make it home."

Home.

To New York.
Where she belongs.

Kate might think he was a coward, and the hurt look on her face made him feel like one, but the truth was she couldn't stay here. Even if he wanted her to. She had a life in the city. He wasn't going back to New York. All that was left for him there was a lengthy legal battle. A few what-the-hell-happened-to-you interviews. And family, he reminded himself. *His* family.

Jake glanced down at their interwoven fingers. He'd always been a fixer, the guy who held on and made relationships work. Even the wrong relationships. Especially the wrong ones. But he didn't believe in relationships anymore. And he wasn't interested in love.

The island was home now.

Even if she was right. Even if he *was* hiding.

Kate stopped at the edge of the cove and turned toward him, her eyes clear and bright. "Just so you know. I'll always remember today. Thank you for bringing me here. For sharing your personal fantasy." Her skin flushed that sweet, pretty pink. "For the overnight accommodations. But mostly, for all the really hot chips." She smiled up at him, casually beautiful, but more than *just* beautiful. *So much more.*

After pressing a soft kiss on his lips, she turned to go, and as he watched her drift toward the stone stairs, that dull ache settled squarely in the middle of his chest. Maybe he'd managed to avoid becoming Cupid's next target, enjoyed one helluva night, not to mention one heavenly morning. But watching her walk away, a thought struck him as hard as a storm wave, the kind with the power to knock a guy sideways.

Even when her first shot missed its mark, Cupid almost always got the last laugh.

The Daily Blog: Smart Cupid.com.
Posted by Senior Love Blogger, Kate Bell.

Let's face it, Cupids, we've all been there. Wild, impulsive actions in an extreme situation (for example, flying into a hurricane), leading to flirtatious behavior (with a man, who may or may *not* be a hottie, but who is *definitely* your interview), followed by spontaneous kissing, and before you know it…a one-night fantasy.

Now, I am *not* recommending this for every situation, every man, or every relationship. I believe in commitment. But not every guy has to be the right guy. Not every guy is The One.

So.

If a chance to enjoy some mind-blowing, life-altering fantasy sex just *happens* to come along…well… frankly, a one-night, no-strings-attached, side dish of man candy may be desirable. Even healthy.

Think of it as a sweet, sexy stop along the road to self-actualization. True, the morning after will likely be… awkward. Even a bit painful. *Do not hyperventilate. Do not run.* Take a deep, seven-second breath, and on the exhale, get out of bed (make the bed—good form if you're a guest), check the weather (you *did* fly into a hurricane), and then, wearing your heart on the strap of a borrowed bikini, find your bachelor (the object of your inappropriate flirtatious behavior).

For better or worse, some memories simply can't go on the record. Keep those close, enjoy the last of your sexy times, and kiss him good-bye. Because while a twenty-four hour fantasy *can* restore a girl's confidence and help heal her broken heart, an island fantasy is not forever. Climb onto the plane (or subway or bus) bound for home and get back to the business of living *your* life.

Pursue your own career. Make *your* dreams the priority. But keep your heart open. Even if it stays empty for a while, eventually, when you least expect it, The One will find you.

Let him.

Chapter Nine

Six weeks later...

Kate raced for the A Train. Late again, she shoved a stale breakfast bar down her throat. The grime and humid air of the Brooklyn subway clung to her black linen dress. Crazy, but she loved this city. After elbowing past the other Manhattan castaways to the back of the car, she settled into a corner and turned up the volume on her iPod. Anything to free her mind from fixating on what would happen now that her bachelor profile had tanked.

Or more accurately, now that she'd insisted it not be published. Jake didn't want to be Smart Cupid's next bachelor any more than she wanted to go back to Ohio, so she'd bailed on the profile—which meant no *Cosmo*.

She wanted to be New Kate, free from obsessing over what tomorrow would bring, but without that job, she'd scarcely be able to afford her rent-controlled apartment. A fact her father would remind her of as soon as she told him.

At the next platform, the subway doors rattled open,

and more commuters crammed onto the train. The space expanded to accommodate them like a clown car. "Next station, Columbus Circle," a mechanized voice announced as the train lurched forward. Kate's shoulder slammed against a dingy yellow poster plastered on the back wall. Fifteen minutes, three subway stops, and two blocks later, she strolled into the office to find her boss standing in reception, a Starbucks cup in one hand and a pink envelope in the other.

Her stomach contracted. *Pink-slipped. Fired.* Jane never waited for anyone in reception. Hell, the woman ran on caffeine, adrenaline, and candy. Waiting wasn't in her skill set. But there she was, waiting in reception. *Definitely about to be fired.* Kate drew in a breath and braced for it. She was prepared, self-actualized. She could handle anything.

As usual, her boss got straight to the point. "*Cosmo* called."

Not what she'd expected, but better, much better. "*Cosmo* — as in — the *magazine*?"

Jane offered a quick nod and handed her the Starbucks cup, probably a consolation latte to let her down easy. *At least I'm not about to be fired.* "Don't get me wrong," Jane said, "I'm still disappointed that you pushed for us to not publish the profile, but I actually kind of respect you for it. I love my brother, and after the shit he's been through, I'm glad someone else cares about him, too. But more to the point, you actually got him to agree to do the interview. So when you got back from Paradise, I emailed your bachelor profile."

Kate clutched the green-and-white cup. Despite her six questions and perfect context for a romantic write-up, she'd come back to work and made a case for tanking the profile. Jake wanted his peace. Whether they were good or not, he had his reasons for staying away from Manhattan, and she didn't want to be the one who dragged him back. She understood. Some experiences *are* private, not meant for Facebook or

Instagram.

She looked back at her boss. "But you agreed not to run the profile."

"And I didn't," Jane said with a shrug of her shoulder. "I simply emailed the draft, along with your follow-up blog post, to my friend at the magazine."

Her nerve endings fired on all cylinders. "And?"

Jane flashed her patented grin. "And she liked it. So much that she wants you to write a spec piece for her." She held out the envelope, still pink but clearly emblazoned with the *Cosmo* logo. "The contract is in here, pretty straightforward. You've got three days to send her a brand new article, and if she loves it, the job is yours."

"Oh my God, Jane, thank you!" This was it—her second chance of a lifetime. She reached for the envelope, but her boss's grip tightened on its edges.

"There's just one teeny tiny issue…not related to the piece, not *exactly*…" She paused for a full thirty seconds before blurting out her one teeny tiny hitch. "Jake's coming to town."

Her grip on the envelope tightened, wrinkling its crisp edges. She took a seven-second breath. Cleared her throat. "But I thought he'd never—"

"Come home? To the city? I know; me, too." Jane let go of the envelope like the thing had burst into flames. "But in the middle of last night, a water line broke open in his kitchen…"

She gave herself a mental shake. "His *kitchen*."

Jane gave a short nod. "Ruined the hardwood floors, which is a problem, since the place is currently in escrow, and *yes*, he asked me to hire a contractor to do the repairs to make sure the deal stays together, and I *did*, but now the contractor can't finish the job, some kind of family emergency, so I was *hoping* you'd be able to complete the repairs before he gets here."

Her palm smoothed the line of her new pencil skirt, shooting for casual, probably missing the mark completely. "And when does he arrive?"

"Well…" Jane bit down on her bottom lip. "Tomorrow."

"*Tomorrow?*" Her breath caught in her throat. Yes, her time on the island had been an adventure, but seeing him *here*, in *New York,* where she *lived,* in her city, her home, where she might actually fall for the man.

Jane gave her a curious look. "Is that a problem?"

Kate drew in a deep breath to realign her ch'i. It had been painful to walk away from him, and maybe that was part of why she'd sacrificed the profile. To prove to herself she was different. The *new* new Kate, a super-smooth (maybe) *Cosmo* girl who'd enjoyed a one-night, one-afternoon romance, experienced the mystery of multiple orgasms, and walked away without expectation. *No strings, no regrets.*

"No problem." Kate offered a beatific smile, not wanting her friend to see that she'd felt rattled—*slightly* rattled—by the imminent arrival of her ex–island romance.

Her friend peeked over the rim of the coffee cup. "Maybe Jake could give you some kind of exclusive, you know, for the spec piece."

She shoved the paperwork into her tote. "I thought we were respecting his privacy?"

"Kate, he doesn't want people to think of him as an eligible bachelor, but that doesn't mean he can't do an interview about the book that made him famous. *Cosmo* is giving you a shot, but you need to come up with something that will *wow* them. What could be better than twenty-first century advice from a relationship expert?"

She bit down on her bottom lip. "I don't know. He's already turned down the bachelor profile."

"So find another angle," Jane continued with a wave of her coffee cup. "Take him to dinner. Pin him down. Ask a few questions, and before he knows what hit him, you've got a red-hot exclusive you can use to wow them over at *Cosmo*. You've got this."

"A red-hot exclusive." Her mouth twisted to one side. This was it. Her dream on the line. But the words "red-hot" and "Jake Wright" sent her pulse racing, and he wasn't even in the room.

"He owes you for not publishing the bachelor profile."

Kate shook her head. "No, he…"

"If it was up to me, he'd be Smart Cupid's Most Eligible, so…" Jane reached out and gave her hands a squeeze. "Trust me, he owes you." She turned and walked toward her office. "*Big time.*"

Jane was right. If she wanted her dream job at *Cosmo*, she needed something special. From a professional standpoint, Jake Wright fit the bill. But on a personal level, could she handle seeing him again? She chewed on her lip. Yes. *Absolutely*. For *Cosmo*, she could absolutely handle him. She needed to meet him on her terms, that's all, preferably dressed in a preppy suit, sitting on the opposite side of a large table in a well-lit restaurant teeming with people, where kissing and everything it led to would be out of the question. Her mouth twisted to one side. Not exactly a bulletproof plan, but yes, she could handle Jake Wright.

In New York. In a carefully controlled setting.

Absolutely.

No problem.

. . .

Jake needed to crash. Standing on the empty sidewalk, he adjusted the weight of the black leather bag from one shoulder to the shoulder and fished the phone from the pocket of his cargos *Damn. 3:50 a.m.* He pressed the bridge of his nose between his fingers. The midnight flight from the island to Manhattan in a cramped puddle jumper had been killer, trumped only by the brutal cab ride that made one thing abundantly clear: he was back in New York. He'd been out of touch with its urban rhythms for a long time, but from Brooklyn through every stop on the Henry Hudson Parkway, the city was still home. Once he settled the issues with the apartment and the new book, he'd head back to the island. But New York would stay with him, for better or worse.

Looking up at the penthouse apartment of his yellow brick and limestone building in Tribeca, he considered calling his sister to see if she'd found someone to fix the floor, but this was not the hour to call Jane. He hoped she'd found a guy, though. If not, the damage to the hardwood would be so extensive they'd need another month for the repairs.

He needed to sell the place. He needed to move on.

As he punched his code into the security system, the numbers felt strange and unfamiliar. He'd been away a long time. *A helluva long time.* But the door clicked open, so he pressed forward and walked through the well-appointed lobby. *Nothing too swanky. Nothing out of place.*

He'd always liked this building. His apartment? Not so much. Not after his ex had overhauled the place with chandeliers in the bathroom and gilt ceilings. He liked it simple. Neutral colors. The hardwood floors. The view.

But the condo was the last piece of their settlement. He'd hung on to the place long enough. Time to let go. He was ready. Sell the apartment. Let his ex have her half and start moving forward. He'd spent the last six weeks going over the past. And writing. Learned a lot. He needed to let go of more than his expectations. He needed to let go of his dreams of what his marriage could have been.

If he wanted a future, he needed to let go of the past.

At the back of the lobby, he stepped inside the glass

elevator. Smooth as silk, he ascended to the penthouse, watching the floors disappear under his feet until the elevator doors opened into the apartment, the place he'd called home a lifetime ago. He stepped into the entry, expecting to be alone. Hell, it was four in the morning. But the place wasn't empty. Classic rock blared from the kitchen. Apparently, Jane had found some guy to take the job, which was great news, even if all he wanted was twelve hours of uninterrupted sleep. But working after midnight? He ran a hand over his clean-shaven jaw. Probably costing him a fortune.

"Hello," he called out. No response came back, thanks in part to the blasting of Zeppelin's "Whole Lotta Love." He dropped his bag in the foyer and walked toward the music. "Hello?" *Still nothing.*

His footsteps echoed on the marble floors as he moved toward the archway that led to the kitchen. The opening was covered with plastic sheeting, so he peeled away where it'd been duct-taped to the wall and slipped through. The staccato sound of a nail gun punctuated the drone of several industrial fans and the pulsating rock music.

Halfway through the kitchen, he caught a glimpse of a woman reflected in the glass along the back wall. A gorgeous, windblown, blonde woman. His brain spun out unexpectedly. His sister had managed to find someone to do his repairs. Not just any someone. *Kate Bell.*

Shit. He'd figured there was a chance he'd run into her in town, but…

Shit, shit, shit.

He'd written this new book as a way to purge her from his system. But seeing her proved he'd done no such thing. His entire body came alive again. He wanted to grab her, touch her, kiss her. All bad—*very* bad—ideas.

He opened his mouth to speak, but she was already spinning around, her eyes rounded in surprise.

"Holy shit, you scared me."

Jake stepped back, hands raised. *Damn, this wasn't what I had in mind. Not at all.* "I didn't know you were back here."

She grabbed a remote and clicked down the volume. "Didn't you hear the music?"

He opened his mouth to speak, but his throat had gone dry. Completely. Totally. Desert in the middle of August. He felt…transfixed. Crazy, considering he'd been an authority on sexuality his entire adult life. Hell, he was writing a whole new treatise on sex and freedom—how to experience romance *without* love—but nothing—*nothing*—had prepared him for the woman standing in front of him, in her white tank top, tiny denim shorts, and studded tool belt.

Sex on the beach is one thing, but holy Freudian fantasies, talk about a dream come to life. He swallowed hard and tried not to stare, but fuck, there was no safe place to look. His brain fell into lockdown. All he could think about was grabbling her by that damned belt, hauling her up against the back wall, and burying himself so deep inside her she'd beg him to make her come.

He ran a hand across his face. Forced his brain back into gear. "Obviously, I knew someone was here, but I never expected—"

"Me? Never expected me?" Hip cocked, she stared over at him, her pulse beating wildly at the base of her throat, the remote dangling against her naked thigh. "Well, I didn't expect you, either. In fact, *you* weren't supposed to be here until morning, which is the whole reason I'm working through the night, so I don't have to—"

Not wanting her to finish that sentence, he crossed the dusty, demolished floor in three long strides, took her face in his hands and kissed her. He backed her against that damn wall of windows and kissed her. Kissed her the way he'd wanted to kiss her, every day, every hour, of the past six weeks. Slowly and completely. Kissed her to tell her that she'd inspired him. To tell he'd missed her. Tell her without words. Tell her with a kiss. To make her know he wanted her.

Still.

Now.

He kissed her.

His first, tender kiss tested its boundaries, slowly delving into the sweetness of her lips. He savored the feel of her body melting against him, the sweetness of her addictive scent, the sizzling heat of a Manhattan summer.

With every ounce of willpower left in him, he shook himself and pulled away from her. "Kate, I'm sorry. I shouldn't have—"

"You're goddamn right you shouldn't have. Who do you think you are?" She looked at him with the intensity of an atomic bomb about to go off. She was either going to kill him or...

She grabbed him and kissed him. Deeply. Completely.

And he kissed her right back.

Chapter Ten

Jake Wright. Here. In the city. In the apartment. Right now. No pinstripes. No restaurant teeming with people. No safety zone of any kind. Sure, since coming home, she'd committed to embracing the new Kate, the super-smooth *Cosmo* girl who was through chasing love, who embraced her freedom. But now he was here. Kissing her up against the windows in his torn-up kitchen.

Her head was spinning. She thought she'd be prepared after six weeks without seeing him or touching him. Six weeks of not allowing thoughts of him into her heart, and now he was here, kissing her senseless, making her forget thinking, making her forget time, or rather, making her feel lost in it.

Lost in him.

His lips moved across hers, nipping, swirling, indulging in her depths, and her mouth returned his exploration with a kind of unexpected desperation. Like she never wanted him to stop.

Clinging to the collar of his linen shirt, she breathed him in. His deep musk and ocean air scent made her head spin.

How could he smell so unbelievably good? In the middle of a New York heat wave. He should smell like Chinese food and scorched blacktop. Instead, his scent seduced her with island memories as hot and seductive as the midnight city air.

Warm lips lingered as he broke the kiss. Capable hands framed her face. Expressive blue eyes smiled down at her, and all of a sudden, she felt like she'd been kicked in the solar plexus. *What happened to cute, sexy Jake?* Where were the glasses? The chinos? The *scruff*? Looking up at him with his jaw clean-shaven, his dark hair neatly trimmed, those blue eyes hypnotic without the Costellos, damn, he was gorgeous. Not just cute. Not just sexy. *Hot.* Heart-stoppingly, stupidly hot in a way that made it hard to breathe. A way that caused her toes to tingle and made the arches of her feet rise in anticipation of kissing him. The kind of hot that meant maxed out credit cards and half-eaten boxes of doughnuts. A self-actualized woman didn't fall for that kind of gorgeous. So why now, after all these weeks, did she want to grab that open collar, drag him into the kitchen and ravish every inch of him? *Dammit.*

She closed her eyes and counted to a cleansing seven. Boundaries. She needed boundaries. Not him showing up without any warning, all cleaned up and dangerously hot in that way that had always brought her nothing but trouble. She was re-focused on her life and career. No more complicated, misguided relationships. *Cosmo* was on the line.

She released her grip on his collar and took a step back. Messing everything up for a guy, who for some unfathomable reason filled her every waking thought, was a mistake. Time to shove this lust-inducing genie deep into his bottle. "You need to leave."

"Leave?" An indulgent smile broke across his face. "Kate, I just stepped off a midnight flight. What I *need* is to crash in my King-sized bed."

King-sized bed. Not only did he *look* more seductive; he *sounded* more seductive, too, his deep, panty-melting voice murmuring about midnight needs and beds large enough to spend a day in. A blush crept across her cheeks. "I don't care what time it is. You can't stroll in here and kiss me in the middle of your kitchen."

"Stroll in here? This is *my* apartment." He gave her a once-over. "What are you wearing, anyway?"

She needed to stay cool and not hyperventilate. "Maybe you've not noticed yet, but it's August here in Manhattan, the AC in *your* apartment is busted, and it's stifling. Why else would I be standing in your kitchen, wearing…"

"Nothing but a tool belt?" he asked with a devilish twinkle in his eyes.

A low sound vibrated in the back of her throat as she stalked past him into the living room. "I have shorts on."

He followed behind her. "Those hardly qualify."

Kate spun around. "You need to go." She yanked her T-shirt from the iron banister, pulled the oversized tee over her head, and tried to keep it together. "Go grab some coffee, or a sandwich, check out the self-help section at The Strand, whatever lifts your sails, but I need two more hours to rip up the last of the warped wood and install your new floor.

He shoved a hand through his hair. "It's the middle of the night."

"And you're not supposed to be here." She shoved her feet into a pair of rhinestone studded flip flops. "Why *are* you here?" she asked, noting how he took in the logo emblazoned across her yellow tee. BELL CONSTRUCTION. *STEEL ERECTION SPECIALISTS.* She cocked an eyebrow and dared him to say a word.

He scrubbed his face with both hands. "I'm here to assess the damage and oversee repairs on the apartment."

"Right." She wrapped her fingers around the doorknob

and yanked open the front door.

He took a step toward the door. "Where are you going?"

"Home. I need to rest, because tomorrow I plan to kill your sister." She tilted her head to one side and stood in the open doorway. "Or maybe I'll do that now. Murder her in her sleep."

"Kate...honestly...this is my fault." Hand still clutching the knob, she turned back slowly. He picked up her discarded tool belt and approached her casually, the way Matt Lauer might move toward a tiger on one of those wild animal segments for the *Today* show. He held out the belt. "Jane had no idea I was flying in early."

"Eagle Scout's honor?"

He held up his right hand. "Eagle Scout's honor."

She accepted the belt and wrapped it around her hips. "You're really selling the condo?"

"I'm *really* selling the condo."

"*Just* selling the condo?" A fully-loaded click of her tool belt punctuated her words. Not that she wanted him to be here for any other reason, but selling the condo, overseeing repairs, finalizing escrow—all could have been managed remotely. So why was he here? *In New York?* Her brows rose expectedly.

Jake dug his hands deep into his pockets. "Actually, I'm making good on the last of my contractual obligations to my agent, or rather, ex-agent."

"Ex-agent." Her words tumbled over his, her question only partially satisfied. "I see."

He shrugged. "New manuscript."

After a short pause, she cleared her throat and continued. "So, you're writing again?"

"Seems I was inspired."

"*Inspired*." She forced herself to take a breath. "To write or—"

"Yes, to write and—"

"—to just walk in after six weeks and kiss me?"

Jake stood still, looking over at her as if he suspected there was a right answer to her question and a wrong one. "Maybe?"

"Maybe. *Maybe?*" To think she recalled her time with him on the island as a romantic, sexy dream. *Maybe.* She pulled her cell from the pocket of her tool belt and autodialed Manhattan Taxi. "I'm calling a cab."

He opened his mouth, probably to try a different answer, but she waved him off and moved toward the door. "No need to explain."

A hand tore through his hair. "I didn't expect to see you here tonight. I didn't mean to…"

"To kiss me? Yes, I got that." Distracted by his hips in those low-slung shorts, she'd hesitated long enough that her hand was only now wrapping around the doorknob.

"Yellow Cab." The dispatcher's heavy New York accent broke through a Muzak version of "Ridin' in My Car."

Jake moved toward the door. "Stay. This is my fault. Let me make it up to you."

"Hey, anybody there?" She pressed the phone against her chest to mute the cabbie's obvious frustration.

She looked back at him, unexpected tears pricking at the back of her eyes. "I'll be back in the morning to finish the floors." She moved to go.

"Kate." His fingers curled around the edge of the doorframe. "Please. *Stay.*"

A deep breath. Her body stilled. Her eyes shut against the pull of that one simple word. *Please.* In all her life, no man had ever asked her to stay the way he was asking. *Please stay.*

He reached out and caught her fingertips, and that simple touch made everything come rushing back. The kisses. The Scrabble. The cove.

Please stay. The words threw her heart into fast-forward,

and she knew that if she looked in his eyes, her last hope for sanity would vanish. Crazy as it seemed, she had missed him. Missed this man she barely knew.

The dispatcher's impatient voice broke through the line. "Honey, this is all peaches and cream, but is there any chance in hell you still need a cab?"

She took a deep breath and met Jake's gaze. He smiled, less sure than she'd ever seen him. "No, I'm sorry…no cab."

"You sure you're okay?" he asked, his tone all New York protective.

Kate smiled into the phone. "Nothing I can't handle."

"'Kay. That changes, you call me back," he said before the line went dead.

Kate tucked the phone into her belt, looked over at Jake, and tried to ignore the way the linen shirt clung to his muscled shoulders. *Damn his busted air-conditioning.* She looked away. Like she'd told the cabbie. Nothing here she couldn't handle.

"I'm sorry," Jake said, stepping away, lowering both hands into his pockets. "I shouldn't have walked in and kissed you that way."

"Yeah. You shouldn't have."

Of course, neither should she.

A nervous feeling settled in her stomach. She closed the door with a quiet click, let go of the knob, and walked over to settle at the bottom of the stairs. Maybe this wasn't how she had planned to see him again. But here she was. No navy suit. No busy restaurant.

On the bottom step of a spiral staircase.

She tucked a piece of hair behind her ear and tried to ignore her heart knocking up against her ribcage. "Good flight?"

He walked over and settled next to her. "Long flight."

She glanced over at him from beneath her lashes and was struck by just how well he cleaned up. "Any martinis?"

He let out a low, sexy chuckle. "No martinis."

"Too bad." He was close enough to kiss again. Close enough to breathe him in. Made it tough to remember that he was just a sweet, sexy stop along the road to self-actualization. "So, what's it about?" His brows rose in question. "The new book."

"Oh, the new book." He appeared startled, as if he'd never imagined telling her, and if not for the leak in the kitchen, he might never have told her. She may have glimpsed the cover through some bookstore window. Picked it up. Remembered their twenty-four hours. Funny to think about how it all worked. Fate. Karma. *Luck*.

He ran a hand over his jaw. "Let's call it a modern take on adding romance to your life."

Kate bit down on her lip. Talk about one hell of an exclusive. "Something along the lines of *The Romance Factor?*"

An easy shrug of his perfect shoulders. "More along the lines of…defining contemporary relationships." He pushed up his sleeves. *Wow, even his forearms are better than I remembered.* "Never had a chance to thank you for not splashing me all over in Internet in my boxer briefs."

Now was her chance. If she wanted to be taken seriously… well, here was her opportunity. "How do you feel about an exclusive?"

"Exclusive?"

"An interview for the book," she raced ahead, "and before you shut me down, this would be a strictly promotional, non-personal, non-matchmaking article."

"No bachelor-of-the-month, win-a-date-with-Jake Wright madness?"

"No bachelor-of-the-month, win-a-date-with-Jake Wright madness."

He nodded slowly, deliberating. "But we'd spend time

together."

"Researching the article—yes." *Best to establish the rules up front.* "All business, nothing personal.

He gave her an assessing look. "Three days. All business. Nothing personal."

"Three days?"

"That's how long I plan to be in New York."

Kate held her breath and shoved aside her twinge of disappointment. If this was business, his timeline worked perfectly. An exclusive interview with the up-until-now reclusive Jake Wright was the definition of "the un-gettable get." The kind that made careers. In three days, she could have a knockout piece that practically guaranteed her the job at *Cosmo.*

"Deal?" He bumped her shoulder with his, like a kid sitting on the curb with his neighborhood girlfriend, and extended his hand. Like it was simple.

But was a deal with an ex-lover ever simple? She'd had her heart broken so many times, but her career depended on this exclusive. Besides, she was the new Kate. Realigning her ch'i. Focusing on her life. Letting love find her.

And avoiding it in the wrong places.

"Deal—for *Cosmo* girls everywhere." No time for second thoughts, she slipped her hand into his, and a familiar sense of kismet—*non-martini infused kismet*—rocked her insides. Clearly, her ch'i was already cracking. Even so, she'd gotten the exclusive. Now, if she was smart, she'd get the hell out of there before her biorhythms went totally out of whack and she felt inspired to kiss him again. She shoved her hand into her back pocket and turned to go. "We can start in the morning."

"Whoa, wait a sec." Jake caught her elbow. "In the morning?"

"In the morning." Kate glanced at his hand, wondering when her elbow had become an erogenous zone. "I'll be here at seven."

"Kate, no. It's already almost four-thirty. You'll barely have time to get home before you have to turn right back around."

"I'm not sure I see an alternative."

"Sure you do. Stay here."

Her gaze met his. "Not sure that's such a good idea."

He grinned. "Worried you can't handle me?"

"I'm sure I can." Except she wasn't. "It's you I'm worried about."

He held up his hands in a gesture of surrender. "No funny business from me. You take my bed. I'll take the couch."

She looked at her watch. Damn him, he was right. Half an hour to get home. A shower. Lay down in bed. Then it was time to get back in a cab.

"Fine," she said. No matter how tempting he might be, all cleaned up and good-looking, she was done looking for love in all those sexy, charming, wrong, *wrong* places. Love was going to have to find her. "But this is all business. Nothing else."

Because she'd definitely stopped looking.

Definitely.

For good.

Chapter Eleven

On a what-was-I-thinking scale of one to ten, Kate's late-night deal with Jake topped out somewhere around eleven. Seventy-two hours spent researching Jake's hot new theory. And no hanky panky? What had she been thinking? That she could spend three sex-free days with the man? She lined up another piece of the hardwood and set the mallet against the edge.

Hell, the past seven hours had sent her senses reeling. Memories of their time on the island had kept her tossing and turning. In his bed. Alone. *Damn.* She slammed the mallet too hard against the plank. From across the half-completed floor, Jake flashed one of his wicked smiles. *Like he knows exactly what I'm thinking.*

She looked back at him, annoyed by the effect his smile had on her, irritated by the overly-meticulous way he lined the next floorboard. "Oh my word," she said, losing her cool. "We're installing a floor, not performing brain surgery. For crying out loud, put the tongue in the groove and bang it." She slammed another plank into place. Clearly, all those deep breathing exercises were not helping.

His smile widened, all flirtatious and gorgeous. "Think I'll stay with slow and easy."

She rolled her eyes. "I was talking about the floor."

He angled his mallet against the side of the board. "I thought you meant—"

"I didn't." She banged a piece of hardwood into place. Let him be as flirtatious as he wanted. She was through with making relationships more significant than they actually were. *No more bad dates. No more half-assed relationships.*

"Kate, can you give me a hand with this?" he asked, tapping the mallet into the board. "This one won't connect."

She pinned him with a suspicious look. "I thought you renovated the floors in your bungalow."

He leaned back on his haunches, and the faded denim of his jeans stretched across the muscles of his thighs in a way that made her feel like she might melt into the floor. Or possibly say the hell with it all, grab him by the collar, and pick up where they left off last night.

"I refinished those floors. Installation is a whole different technique." He smiled. *Okay, definitely melting into the floor.* "Of course, I'm more than willing to learn a new technique." The way he said it could mean more than a simple home renovation tutorial, but she needed to keep her eye on her exclusive.

No. No way he meant that. They'd agreed this wasn't going anywhere beyond business.

"Let's stick with the basics." She slid across the floor to settle next to him.

He eased closer. "I like the basics."

I bet you do, she thought. After slipping a tapping block from her tool belt, she leaned forward and placed the block against the side of the floorboard. "See how the groove in the block aligns with the tongue of the plank to give it a cushion?

Makes it less likely to cause damage. Some blocks have multiple groove lengths. Others have ball-shaped handles."

She reached for another piece of hardwood and tried not to think about the fact that he was the hottest-looking guy she'd laid her eyes on—ever.

"So how's dating going now that you're the new Kate?"

She slammed the mallet down. Hard. "That's really none of your business."

"You think I'm trouble," he said.

"I *know* you're trouble."

His smile widened. "Just wondering how the new you is working out. You know I'm rooting for you." He raised his eyebrows. Shot over his persuasive sweet, charming smile. "Don't want you to miss an opportunity to be spontaneous."

Her tongue dashed out to wet her lips. "Spontaneous?"

He grinned, clearly aware of the effect he was having on her with his talk about dating and spontaneity. "A woman ready to dive into a new spur-of-the-moment adventure is sexy."

She ignored the sudden rush of heat flooding through her. "This from a man who overpacks a picnic and meticulously measures his floorboards."

A low, impossibly sexy laugh rumbled up from his chest. "Maybe I know the value of caution, but I also know there's something sensual about embracing the unexpected. Letting go."

Letting go. Exactly what she was trying to do—*let go*. She focused her attention back on the damn the floor, but her heart was pounding so hard, she wondered if he could hear it. "And how does this *exclusive lesson* apply to installing a new kitchen floor?"

She slammed the mallet down—right onto her thumb. She dropped the mallet and sprang onto her feet, yelping curses.

He came after her, held up his hands, waiting for her to calm down. "Come here, come here, come here."

Her whole hand throbbed with pain. She cradled it in her other hand. "I'm an idiot."

He took her hands into his. Soft touch. So soft. "No, it's my fault. I kept trying to get under your skin."

She glared at him. "So you admit it."

"Old habits die hard. And you're so much fun when you're angry. Let me see."

She swallowed, closed her eyes, and opened her hands, afraid of what she'd see. "Is it bad?"

"Well...we might have to amputate."

She opened her eyes and glared at him. "Still joking—"

He rubbed her injured hand with his palms. "It's fine. Maybe a little bruise."

Already, the pain was subsiding. And his touch was leaving something very troublesome in its place. "Stop that. My hands are dirty."

"My hands are dirty, too. Does that feel better?"

It did. A lot. Too much.

He brought his hand to her mouth and kissed it. Her body shuddered. What a mess. But it left her hungry for his touch. He lowered her hand and started to turn away.

"Jake..."

It was all the invitation he needed. His lips brushed hers, a fleeting touch that left her wanting more, so she pulled his mouth down to hers, kissing him completely, and the torn-up kitchen fell away. Call it *spontaneous*. Call it *research*. She didn't care. She breathed him in, all spicy soap and fresh laundry. She wanted the feel of his lips on hers, kissing her until she literally thought her heart might explode into hundreds of pieces. She could barely breathe, barely string two thoughts together.

The vibration of her phone against her hip reverberated

through the fog of her thoughts. She tried to ignore it, but the damn thing kept buzzing. Reaching for the place where it was hooked into her tool belt, she felt Jake's fingers skim down her arm, searching for the phone.

"Oh God, please," he whispered against her mouth, "don't answer."

"I have to answer." The phone kept buzzing and buzzing and buzzing, so she shifted away from him, pulled the phone from the compartment on her tool belt and answered without looking at the screen. "Kate Bell."

Jane's voice echoed through the phone. "I'm on my way."

Kate struggled to keep her tone even and calm. The last thing she wanted was to give her friend the slightest hint she was breathless, that moments ago, she'd been dangerously close to a round of spontaneous research.

"On your way where?" Jake dropped a kiss on her shoulder, and she waved him away.

"To Jake's place," she said in her direct way. "When you didn't turn up at the office, I figured you were still working, and since I owe you for the floors…"

She stared at the phone, her head already shaking no. This was a disaster waiting to happen. The last thing she needed was for her friend to arrive, find out her brother had arrived early, and get any new matchmaking ideas. "Jane, I don't think that's such a good idea."

There was a short pause as if she'd thrown her for a loop, and then, "Coffee's always a good idea."

"Normally, I'd agree with you, but…we're just banging away over here." She sent Jake a pleading look. "No need to stop by." Jake fell back against the floor and groaned. Too late, she realized her mistake. Not only was she a dating disaster, but she was a terrible liar.

"We?" Sharp as the edge of a backsaw, Jane pressed for more information. "Who's we?"

Kate raised her eyes to the ceiling and scrunched up her face, readying for the blow. "Me…and your brother."

"Jake?" Her voice leaped an octave. "He wasn't supposed to get here until this afternoon. Let me talk to him." Kate shot him another pleading look, and he held his hand out for the phone.

While he spoke with his sister, Kate smoothed the line of her T-shirt, straightened her tool belt, grateful they'd been interrupted mid-kiss, mid-whatever. Because all that action in the middle of his kitchen floor might have been *spontaneous*, but it also defined the words "close call." Kate shoved the tapping block into its compartment and yanked on the belt, wondering why the hell she'd kissed him in a way that clearly violated her own rules. Chalk it up to the fact that the sex between them had been amazing and sweet and tender.

No—he was off-limits. The man didn't believe in love. And she didn't want to screw up her last chance to save her career. She'd sacrificed the bachelor profile for him. But this exclusive? He owed her. And she meant to claim.

She eyed him as he wrapped up the call, an easy smile on his face. For better or worse, she liked him. Liked his ocean blue eyes. Liked his clean scent. Liked the impossibly enticing grin that made her want to confess all her fantasies. And then share them on the kitchen floor. *Close call?* Absolutely.

Finished with the call, Jake moved the phone back and forth between them. "This lesson is not over," he said, handing her the cell. "But I have to go. I have a meeting with my publisher in an hour, and thanks to my sister's ability to call at the most inconvenient time," he said, shaking his head in affectionate surrender, "I've got to swing by the Smart Cupid office, too." He shook his head and sighed. "Do you have plans for lunch?" he asked.

"You tell me."

"We can at least go over what you want the interview to

look like."

"Are you sure that's all we're going to talk about?"

He smiled. "We can talk about that kiss if you want, but I know we said this would be all business."

He had a point. A stolen kiss wasn't such a big deal as long as they ignored it.

Yeah, Kate. That's a brilliant strategy.

"Deal."

. . .

Fishing the phone from the pocket of his shorts, Jake looked up at the corner office of the sleek building in the Flatiron. He turned the phone over and considered calling Jane. Let her know he'd cut his meeting short and arrived early. But—no. So much more fun to be a surprise.

A few minutes later, armed with her favorite extra hot, no-whip, triple mocha latte, he stepped out of the elevator and walked down the hall into the Smart Cupid offices. Nice place—bold, sophisticated, cool—just like Janey. He felt a surge of pride in his chest. Yeah, damn proud.

He stopped in front of a small desk overrun with technology, and a pretty, dark-haired woman wearing tortoise-shell glasses blinked up at him. He'd only seen her in a wedding photo. *Nick's wedding photo.* Yeah, he'd missed a lot by staying away. More than he'd counted on.

A pang of guilt in his gut joined his sense of pride as he offered his hand to his brother's newlywed wife. "You must be Marianne. I'm—"

"Jake," she said.

Her voice was warm and sweet. A far cry from Nick's usual type, the ambitious legal eagle looking for a fun Saturday night, and yet, if she was taken aback by his out-of-the-blue arrival, she gave no indication. No doubt she could handle Nick. He liked her immediately.

A conspiratorial smile broke across his face, and he nodded toward the corner office. "Thought I'd get here early. Surprise Jane."

In what could only be a well-practiced stall tactic, she readjusted her glasses against the bridge of her nose. "Maybe I should let her know you're here."

"And spoil the surprise?"

She bit down on her bottom lip. "Not sure she enjoys surprises. Statistically speaking."

Jake's smile widened into a grin. He knew exactly how much his sister liked a good stunner. "Not even a little? Not even when I come bearing coffee?"

"Not even a little." She eyed his misguided coffee-flavored peace offering and lowered her voice to a whisper. "And after the whole bachelor fiasco…"

"M.A., can you please…" His sister walked out of her office, nose pointed at a tablet computer, forehead wrinkled. He cleared his throat, and she stopped in her tracks.

A knowing smile tugged at the corner of her mouth. "Well, if it isn't Mr. July."

He held his arms out wide. "The one and only."

"Except it's August." The snap of her tablet closing emphasized the point. She walked over and pressed a kiss on his cheek. "I wasn't expecting you for another hour." She flashed him a smile. "But I'm happy you're here."

Jake drew his sister into a bear hug and looked over her shoulder at Marianne.

"Good surprise?" he asked.

Marianne nodded. "Good surprise."

• • •

"A new book?" Jane tore into a bag of peanut M&Ms. "That's

the reason you're here?"

"Not the only reason." Jake eased onto the red velvet sofa a few feet from his sister's oversized desk, stretched out his legs, and crossed them at the ankles. "I get to see my brother and sister and wrap up the sale of the apartment, but yes, there's a new book."

Jane settled into the chair behind her desk. "Three years and, all of a sudden, a new book."

He shrugged. "Easier than digging my heels into a lawsuit against my ex-agent."

His publisher was dealing with that asshole, so as long as Jake delivered the second book on his contract, he'd never have to see him again. *A definite bonus.*

"Easier since when?"

"Since I've been…inspired."

"Inspired." She gave him nothing. A poker face.

Jake shifted slightly. Cleared his throat. He knew she was pissed that he'd bailed on the bachelor interview, even more so that he'd side-stepped her attempted matchmaking, but the truth was, she'd done him a tremendous favor. Kate *had* inspired him. Hell, maybe she was his Muse. "All I know is that the book was banging at my insides, dying to get out."

"So what's the title?" she asked, all nonchalant curiosity.

Yep, here's where it got tricky.

He shifted on the loveseat. "*No Strings Attached*. It explores my new theory that a friends-with-benefits situation is a healthy way to get a guy's groove back."

She leaned back in her chair. "Get a *guy's* groove back?"

"Yes."

"What about a woman?" The tearing of candy wrapper emphasized her words.

His eyes narrowed on the crinkled packaging. *So not static.* "What *about* a woman?"

Jane pinned him with a look like the one she'd used when

they were kids and he'd hidden the beat-up, stuffed monkey she'd loved. "Can a friends-with-benefits *situation* help to get a *woman's* groove back?"

He arched a brow. "I don't see why not."

Jane nodded. "And after the *groove* is *back*?"

He folded his arms over his chest. "Nothing. That's the beauty of it. In the contemporary dating landscape, a 'friends-with-benefits relationship' is the new gold standard."

"The *contemporary* landscape? The *gold standard* of relationships?" Jane laughed as if she knew the punch line of a joke he hadn't quite figured out. "You call that inspired?"

The muscles in his jaw clenched defensively. "This is a strong, psychologically valid theory about how nice guys—and, *yes,* nice women—can have a short-term sexual relationship and enjoy it. Not everyone needs a commitment to be complete. Life's not a Tom Cruise movie." He'd learned that one the hard way. *Marriage Lesson Number One.* He leaned back on the couch. "There's joy in freedom."

"Sounds like a lot of bullshit to me." She tossed a few of the candies into her mouth and gave him a long, assessing look. "Yep, this is better than I expected. I can't wait to tell Nick."

"Tell him what?" Jake suspected his sister's attitude had something to do with Kate, but he'd already explained that her matchmaking radar was way off on that score.

She picked up her cell and pressed the speed-dial. "Tell him you're on the ropes."

"I am not on the ropes."

A mischievous laugh escaped her. "Okay, Jake, if you say so."

"I am—" Jake drew in a breath. *Not on the ropes.*

"By the way, I spoke with Kate about her exclusive." She shifted forward, a smile edging across her face. "Since she's too nice to call you on it, I asked legal to draw up the contract."

She opened up her drawer, took out a lengthy document, and tossed it onto the desk. "Sign it. Give it to Kate." She held up the phone to indicate their brother had picked up—and on the first ring or two. He never picked up that fast for him. "Nick, guess who's in my office." She covered the phone with her palm. "Should I put him on speaker?"

Jake shook his head. One of them heckling him was enough. As his sister joked with Nick, he picked up the contract. All pretty standard, he thought, burying it into the front pocket of his cargos. But why did she need a contract? Granted, he hadn't described his full-on theory. Or told her the title yet. But he would. Timing was everything. As for the contract, he'd given his word, and he *always* kept his word.

Jake gave his sister the high sign to let her know he was heading out and walked over to the door.

"Where are you running off to?" she asked, ending the call. "I thought we could all grab lunch at *Salvatore's*?"

He leaned his shoulder against the doorjamb. "The old pizza joint in Brooklyn?"

Jane held up the phone. "Nick's in, too."

Damn, he loved that old place down on Washington Street, with its unmistakable red-and-green sign that lit up half the block. He loved Sally, too. The pizza maker with the heavy Brooklyn accent had been more like a father to them than their own. Hell, he'd given Jane a job when they'd needed the money. How many times had the old guy let his sister sneak him slices of pizza out the back door? Probably would have starved if not for Sally. He'd have to get over there before he left the city. "I can't. I made plans to take Kate to Chinatown for lunch."

She tucked her dark hair behind both ears and leaned forward on her elbows. "Spicy Village?'

"Is there any place else?" Jake walked back and gave her a fast kiss on the cheek. "Tell Nick I'll call him later."

She smiled up at him. "After your date?"

"Business," he reminded her, making a break back to the office door. "Not a date."

"If I didn't know better, I'd say you were you definitely on the…"

He stopped in the doorway and looked over at her. "Don't say it."

Jane held back a smile. Gave him a little wave. "Have fun on your date."

Jake turned to go. "Not a date."

Nope. No matter what his matchmaking, date-obsessed sister had to say, he was so *not* on the ropes.

Chapter Twelve

"Now this is New York," Jake said, diving into a Styrofoam container of hand-pulled noodles and shredded chicken in a satisfyingly sauce with hints of beer and chilies, flecked with Sichuan peppercorns. "Remember when you asked me what I missed about New York?" He pointed at the container with his chopstick. "Spicy Big Tray Chicken. New York pizza is fine, but there's nothing like Spicy Big Tray Chicken." He worked the chopstick like a pro. "I may be in love with this chicken."

Kate rolled her eyes. "Not exactly the angle I need for my exclusive."

"But you like it? The restaurant?"

"Like it?" she said. "No. I love it, and the food is amazing." She loaded up her chopstick with a dumpling. "How did you find this place?"

Jake looked around at the definitive hole in the wall: a narrow sliver of a space that let in almost no natural light and boasted less than ten tables. "After I found out about my ex, I had some trouble sleeping. It was tough. My parents' marriage failed to inspire. I wanted something different. Something real. Something that would last."

"Makes sense," she said, chopsticks hovering above the food.

He shrugged. "Guess I wasn't always incapable of a relationship. Uninterested in love."

"Everyone's interested in love."

A small smile crept up on him. "Yeah, some love blogger told me that once. Wonder what ever happened to her."

His smile widened as her napkin hit him square in the face.

"So how does this relate to finding Spicy Village? Food's amazing, but it isn't exactly easy to find." She looked out the window at the narrow street, red and gold lanterns obscuring the view of the graphitized doorways across the way.

"Well, as I said, I'd been having trouble sleeping. Bed at two in the morning. Up at five." A blinking red light over the wall-sized menu caught his attention, then fizzled and burned out. A bit like his marriage, he thought. He looked back at Kate. "One day I said the hell with it. Threw on some clothes and started walking. Everywhere. Central Park. Over Delancey. Down Canal. I ended up in Chinatown, exhausted, outside of this place."

Kate gave him a sympathetic nod. "Of course."

He liked how comfortable she seemed here. His ex-wife never would have stepped into Chinatown, much less Spicy Village. Too bad, because she was missing out on some of the best food in the city. "Must've looked like shit, because the owner opened up early and made me a skillet of his best dish." He pointed toward the chicken. "So I kept coming back. Now he keeps my standing order framed behind the counter."

"Really?" she asked with a smile.

"Really. He was a good friend when I needed one. Wish he was here so I could introduce you," he said, scooping the noodles into his mouth.

She looked at him, a smile at the edges of her kissable mouth. "Well, no wonder."

The gentle sound of her voice washed over him. "No wonder what?"

She reached across the table and laid her hand on top of his, a gesture so much more personal than business. "No wonder you love it so much."

. . .

Thirty minutes later, they stood outside on the sidewalk. The midsummer sun washed the neighborhood in light, reflecting off the boldly-colored signs of Chinatown's narrow shops and stalls selling T-shirts, perfume, jewelry, and "luxury" handbags. The staccato sound of the Mandarin mixed in with the rush of cars and the ding of bells of the bicycle delivery guys. The energy, the sounds, the people. This was why she'd wanted to stay in New York.

"Do you have to go?" Jake asked, casually linking his fingers through hers.

Kate smiled at him, enjoying the feel of him. "No."

"No work deadlines?"

"Just researching my exclusive." For a split-second that shuttered look crossed his face, tension formed at the edge of his eyes. "But if you need to be somewhere…"

"No." His response was quick and certain. "The only place I want to be right now is here with you."

"Me, too." Kate gave his hand a quick squeeze. "Let me take you somewhere," she said, nodding toward the restaurant window. "You shared one of your secret places. I want to share one of mine. So we'll be learning each other's secrets."

He raised an eyebrow. "More research?"

"Absolutely," she said, tugging him down the sidewalk.

"Where are we going?"

"You'll see."

As they crossed over to Canal, they wandered onto a few side streets lined with awnings and flags with Chinese writing, and stopped to buy some ginger, some teas, and a small red plastic Buddha, which she insisted would be good luck. Over on Mulberry, the sweet scents of Lung Moon Bakery seduced them inside, where they loaded up on inexpensive pineapple cakes and lemon and ginger cookies. As they approached Columbus Park, she was already polishing off her second dessert.

She dusted some sugar from her fingers and pointed toward the center of the park where a few people practiced Tai Chi. "Always wanted to come down here and learn Tai Chi."

"Why haven't you?" he asked.

"Just haven't made it down to that place on my list yet." She tilted her chin toward a group of old-timers gathered for intense games of poker and Chinese Chess. "I want to learn mahjong, too."

Jake laughed, and the sound sent her heart racing. "You have a list?"

She nodded. "A New York City bucket list. One of the things I love most about the city is how it's so filled with…"

"Possibility?"

"Exactly," she said, as the sounds of Chinese opera drifted toward them from the park. "Possibility."

Near the end of Canal, she took his hand. "This is what I wanted to show you." She looked over at a yellow brick building with a red and green tile facade. "The Mahayana Temple, and no, I'm not Buddhist," she continued with a smile. "I'm a good Presbyterian girl from a small town in Ohio." She let go a smile. "But it's a beautiful, peaceful oasis. There's so much chaos in the city, and it's all wonderful, but sometimes it's important to unplug and connect."

He looked doubtful. "A Buddhist temple located beneath a billboard for the local casino."

She tugged him up the stairs. "Don't knock it until you try it."

"Am I going to have to meditate?"

"Meditation isn't required, but it is an active place of worship, so be on your best behavior."

He stepped in front of her, snaked his arm around her waist, and pulled her into a kiss that sent her mind reeling. Right there on the steps of the temple. Next to the gold lions.

"I think I better add to my bucket list," she said in a voice she scarcely recognized.

Funny, but he seemed as surprised as she was by his kiss. He nodded toward the entrance. "C'mon, let's get this over with."

"Hey, I tried your big chicken," she whispered as they moved into the temple.

"That's because Spicy Big Tray Chicken is amazing."

Kate gave him a look that said he could go ahead and talk tough, but she noticed his hushed voice as he took in the red and gold foyer. He was open to the experience. Funny, she'd never brought any other man she'd dated here. In some way, she felt able to reveal herself to him. He felt inexplicably safe. She felt his hand low on her back as he ushered her past the foyer. A nice guy in a naughty, *naughty* package.

Inside the temple, the walls were lined with paper strips bearing prayers along with offerings of flowers, fruit, and incense. Kate let the distinctive scent of lotus blossom fill her senses as she took in the magnificence of the temple. Never failed to amaze her. "Beautiful."

His hand at her hip drew her closer. She looked up, and he was gazing down at her as if she, not the temple, was the most beautiful thing he'd ever seen. Her heart did an inappropriate flutter, kicking up a notch at the memory of the way he kissed.

But he was leaving in two days. *Two days.* She bit down on her lip. And yet, her crazy, super-sized heart still wished for more.

Smiling up at him, she took his hand. "Come with me."

Together they walked into the main sanctuary, where an enormous golden seated Buddha looked over the wooden benches. To the right, several visitors milled around a small shrine of boxes filled with scrolls of white paper. "Do you have a dollar?" she whispered.

"A dollar?"

"For a fortune."

He reached into his back pocket. "I don't believe in fortune-telling."

"For a therapist, you are remarkably grounded."

He handed her a twenty. "For an independent woman, you are remarkably light on cash."

"Credit is easier," she said, noting the twenty. "This is too much."

"Consider it a donation to the upkeep of the temple." He pressed the money into her hand. "You need to carry some cash. For safety purposes."

Kate smiled up at him before sliding the donation into the box. "You really are a boy scout. Okay, now, close your eyes and pick one of the *o-mikuji.* "

"The *o-mikuji?*"

A soft laugh escaped her. "*O-mikuji,*" she repeated. "Unrolling the paper reveals the fortune written on it, but you can't think too much. The random quality is purposeful. Simply choose one."

With a skeptical expression on his heartbreakingly handsome face, he pulled a scroll from the box nearest the bell. She reached into a different box, selected an *o-mikuji*, and took his hand to lead him into a quiet corner. "Go ahead, open it," she said in a hushed voice.

Jake unraveled the scroll to reveal two Chinese letters.

Kate peeked over his shoulder and pointed at the symbols. "The first one is a blessing. The second defines your fortunes regarding specific aspects of your life. You've received a half blessing in the area of *tabidachi*, which is travel."

His eyes narrowed. "And what about you? What is your fortune?"

"I thought you didn't believe in fortunes." Kate slanted him a look of anticipation and unrolled the paper as her heart fluttered with a kind of hopeful expectation. Never failed. She loved this place. He slipped his arm around her waist, and the warmth of his hands at her hips sent a different kind of hopeful expectation through the southern regions of her body. Behind her now, he looked down at the paper, waiting for her translation. "Well, mine is a great blessing…" Her voice trailed off, nearly a whisper. "For the fulfillment of my *negaigoto*. My dearest wish. My desire."

His strong fingers tightened at her hips, angling her closer, and moved them deeper into the corner. She turned slowly in his arms. The shadows of this hidden corner played across his handsome face. He opened his mouth to speak, but she pressed her fingers to his lips. Maybe the heady scent of incense was making her light-headed, but she wanted to kiss him. *Now. Right now.* In this beautiful, sacred place, knowing it was as close to a promise as she'd get from this gorgeous man. She reached up and brought his lips down to hers, kissing him like she wanted him to know her wish. Like she wanted him to understand how much she desired him. *Trusted him.* Her lips moved over his, tender and yielding as he returned the kiss, giving as much as taking. Kate poured everything into that kiss, everything she couldn't say, knowing he'd be leaving. But not knowing how she'd be able to let him go a second time. She drew away slowly, lingering in that kiss, a kiss she knew she'd never forget.

Yeah, he wasn't offering love. But she knew who she was.

Where she was. What she had. And this—he—was pretty good.

She just wondered if this would be enough.

"Thank you," she said, her breath heated and shallow, "for coming here with me."

An uncertain expression imprinted on his heartbreakingly handsome face, and he took her face in his hands. "Heck of a wish," he whispered.

Kate grinned up at him. "Heck of a wish."

Chapter Thirteen

As Jake climbed the endless stairs from the sidewalk up to Kate's walk-up apartment, the same question that had been on his mind all day muscled its way back to the forefront. *What the hell am I doing?* He was an island guy. She was a city girl. Relationships were her deal. He'd already tried and failed. But every minute of the day with her had been amazing. Interesting and challenging and *fun*. And every time he kissed her, she felt less like a friend—benefits or no benefits—and more like, hell, he didn't know…a woman he could love.

Which was bullshit, because he was incapable of love. Especially the kind a woman like Kate Bell needed. How had she described it? Star-spangled, bell-ringing love.

Of course, she'd been heavily influenced by martinis at the time, but still. He was pretty sure she meant it. And after that kiss in the temple. He paused to check how many more flights he had to go and tried to shake off the memory, but that was one hell of a kiss. Sexy, yes. Illicit even, but more. Deeper. More than a simple benefit.

Shit. This was not him. He was a guy incapable of

succeeding in a long-term relationship. Emotionally closed off. Uninterested. Whatever the reason. He stopped to look up. Two more flights to go. *Damn, August in the city is hot.*

Maybe that was the answer. The *city*. Back here. Spending time with her in his old haunts. Now he was in Brooklyn. Just an emotional roller coaster. He felt sure of it. He'd wrap up a plan for marketing the book. She'd finish the floors, nab her exclusive. He'd go back to Paradise. No harm. No foul. Because he didn't want to hurt her, and despite the fact that she'd inspired all these feelings in him, and in a way, their "relationship" had given life to his new theory, he worried that—no matter what she said—Kate needed more. More than he could give.

Outside of her apartment, he took a few breaths. He knocked on the door, still thinking his new theory was on the right track, but one look at Kate standing in the doorway of her Brooklyn walk-up knocked the wind out of him.

"Come on in," she said, leaning on the doorframe in a way that emphasized her curves and made him wonder if two more days with Kate Bell would be enough. "I'm almost ready."

As she disappeared into the back of the small apartment, Jake stepped inside, thinking she looked perfect already. Clad in a black T-shirt dress and the strappy kind of sandal a guy could get addicted to, she looked sexy and adorable in that sweet Midwestern way of hers. Lovely and undone. No jewelry, no so-called bling. Hell, the woman knew the specs on an F-series. A BMW, or worse, a Hummer, wasn't on her radar. He loved that his celebrity status, or current lack thereof, never came up. She'd seemed to care for him when he was just an island guy. She'd be happy with a simple life but deserved the best.

Hell, where did that come from? His heart shifted inside his chest, but he shoved away the short tug of emotion.

Normally, he'd be in control of his feelings, but seeing her right now, looking the way she did, he was back on the damn roller coaster. He let go of a low whistle, watching her work her way back into the mostly unfurnished living area.

A pretty flush colored her cheeks. "Ready for a little more research?"

He took a few slow steps in her direction. "I'm thinking we should stay in and delve a little deeper into our original subject," he said, glancing around the walk-up. "You've got a kitchen floor in here, right?"

"My kitchen floor is off-limits."

"How about your closet?" he asked, nodding toward the door off the narrow entry. "Is that off-limits?"

"My *closet*?"

He chuckled, certain her mind was imagining all kinds of kink. He glanced down at the strappy shoes. "Those need to come off." Along with the dress and the red lacy combination he hoped was tucked underneath there. He shook his head in an effort to keep his sexy imaginings at bay. "You need sneakers."

"Sneakers?" she said, glancing down at the shoes,

"I thought we were doing dinner and drinks. Isn't that a traditional contemporary relationship type of date," she said in a rush, as if she was nervous about the kind of alternative date he might have planned. "Or really, it's better to go with just a drink first, and during a quick trip to the ladies' room if a girl gets a friend's approval via Snapchat, then the drink can sometimes lead to dinner. Traditionally."

Jake rolled his eyes. "Women are too complicated." He gave her a pointed look. "Besides you did take me to a Buddhist temple, so maybe I'm thinking I need to step up my game. Better to mix it up a little."

"So we're mixing it up?" Kate sat on her couch, one of a few pieces in the sparsely furnished space and traded her sandals for a cute pair of lace-up sneakers. He shook off the crystal-clear image of his hands skimming across her thighs, caressing those familiar legs.

Get it together, Jake. Hell, the woman's only changing her shoes. "We're mixing it up."

"Sounds like fun." Finished tying on the sneakers, she tossed him a flirty wink that caused more of the long-standing knot in his chest to ease. "So, this place we're going—does it qualify as one of your secrets?"

His brows knit together, not sure what she meant. "My secrets?"

"*Learn Your Partner's Secrets.*" She walked over, her curls cascading around her shoulders, reminding him of how she looked lying beneath him at the cove, her blonde hair fanned out across his old quilt. He shook his head and tried to snap out of it.

"From *The Sex Factor*," she continued. "Your so-called seduction plan. Your list of rules? I mean, I know the exclusive will be on your new book, but I thought linking it to the first would be a cool way to go. Thought I'd open with your rules. *Be Spontaneous, Learn Your Partner's Secrets...*"

Oh, right—his book. His *rules* of seduction.

"No secrets here." He shoved his hands deep into his pockets as a stab of guilt knifed him in the gut. Yes, he'd not told her how his latest theory extolled the virtues of *no-strings attached*, a concept diametrically opposed to her romantic ideals. *Was* he keeping a secret? Not the sexy kind from his book, but the kind that broke people apart. Probably. Did it matter?

Despite the real joy he was finding with her, by the time this next book hit the shelves, he'd be back on the island. Content. Living in peace. He was only in New York to wrap up the sale of the apartment and fulfill his contract. A sexy exclusive with this beautiful, inescapably endearing woman—

not part of the plan. Neither was the way he felt when he looked at her. Or his relentless need to kiss her. His gaze fell to that insanely kissable mouth.

"Intimacy isn't about secrets, or even revelation; it's about the falling away of barriers." Her dress drifted from her shoulder. He lifted it back in place, images of a star-spangled bikini strap and a sun-kissed shoulder filling his thoughts.

He turned her hand over in his. Kissed her palm. Heard her soft intake of breath. "Intimacy is about knowing your partner, her needs and fantasies, and trusting her to know yours."

And damned if he didn't want to know her. Not just one piece of her. *All of her.*

• • •

"Coney Island," she marveled quietly beneath her breath, already anticipating one of her favorite foods in the city. "How did you know I love Coney Island?"

Kate stood near the edge of the amphitheater and gazed up at the dark star-studded sky, as The Romantics rocked out a cool version of "A Night Like This." Perfect song, perfect guy. In fact, she was pretty damn sure tonight was the best night ever. Jake was right; this kind of date was so much more fun than talking finance or business over dinner. *He* was so much more fun, she thought, lifting her face to the moonlit sky. Yes, he was leaving in thirty-six hours, and maybe he wasn't The One, but he was still the best she'd ever had.

"An underrated classic." Jake appeared at her shoulder, carrying two Nathan's hot dogs and a Cherry Coke. The Coney Island special.

She accepted a dog and the soda. "Not your favorite rhythm and blues."

"But The Romantics? Totally my speed." He dove into

the hot dog like a little kid, and Kate's heart melted like the ice in her drink. Last time he was here, he'd shared a day with his dad. One of the last. Kate thought about her parents and knew she was lucky, and her insides ached for him. For the boy he was, and for the gorgeous, guarded man he'd become. One day, she hoped he'd stop hiding. He'd seemed more open this afternoon than she'd ever seen him. Maybe this trip was his first step.

"Best date ever." She took a sip of her soda and gave him a slanted look.

He laughed aloud, and she realized how much she was starting to love that sound. "Not saying much considering you suck at dating."

She bit into the hot dog. "Well, maybe I'm getting better."

He wiped a trace of the spicy mustard from her lip. "I'd bet you were always good."

Gazing up at him, she drew in a breath, counting seven seconds in her head in an attempt to stay focused on her career-first, love-will-find-you platform. Because no matter how sexy his laugh. No matter how fun the time with him felt. She was *this close* to her dream of a *Cosmo* byline coming true. But if she indulged in one night of great sex in Manhattan, would it be so bad? She could have him. At least for one more night. She wanted to be self-actualized, a woman in charge, rather than a woman swayed by charm and music and moonlight, she did, she really, *really* did. But she wanted to kiss him again, too. If she was honest, there was more than kissing on her mind. *So much more.* Could she handle it—another intimate night with him, a falling away of all her barriers?

Or would it wreck her?

As if attempting to answer the question, Jake laced his fingers through hers and gently tugged her away from the edge of the amphitheater. "Ready to up the ante on researching your exclusive?"

Finished with her Coney dog and Coke, she tossed the wrapper into a nearby trash bin. "Depends on what you mean by 'upping the ante.'"

A wicked grin creased his impossibly gorgeous face.

"We're going to test the most important rule of navigating contemporary relationships." He held onto her hand and moved expertly through the nighttime crowd.

Following along as their footsteps fell completely in sync, she gave his hand a squeeze. "What's the most important rule?"

He threw her a smile that spelled trouble. "Be brave."

· · ·

"There's no way I am going on that." Kate took one look at Deno's Wonder Wheel and decided the answer was no—no, no—definitely not.

"Yes, you're taking on The Wheel. Trust me, you'll love it." His hand pressed gently into the small of her back, ushering her forward. "Let's get in line, or we'll miss the best part."

Feet planted on the concrete walkway, she stared up at the beast. "There is no good part about turning circles in a fifteen story wheel of Bethlehem steel."

"This is critical to making your love life more fun."

"A carnival ride?"

"No, being bold, stepping out of the comfort zone."

"I am very comfortable in the zone."

He chuckled and pulled her gently back against his chest. "C'mon, city girl, The Wonder Wheel is a New York landmark, the view from the top is incredible, and it's an amazing piece of construction. Almost one hundred years old, and the Wheel boasts a perfect safety record."

She gave him a slanted look. "Perfect?"

"Perfect." Arms wrapped around her, he marched them

over to the ticket window, "Besides, it's either this or karaoke in the Mermaid Lounge."

"The Wheel it is."

He let out a laugh, a relaxed, happy sound that almost made her think a whirl around the giant wheel was worth it. At the window, Jake let go of her, and she missed the feel of him immediately—the warmth of his chest against her back, the clean and spicy scent of his skin. He plunked down the money for two tickets, and when the pretty twenty-something in the booth gave him a flirtatious smile, a rush of misplaced jealousy ricocheted through her system. Jake turned away and settled his blue gaze on her, his sweet, lingering look making her feel wanted.

He took her hand in his, and they made their way past the smiling clown that beckoned: More Rides This Way. As if they weren't about to step into a gravity-defying death trap.

As they snaked through the line beneath the blue-and-orange steel wheel, Jake kept her hand in his, dropping kisses on her lips, promising caramel apples and cotton candy while Kate tried not to hyperventilate. *Be brave. Why can't revitalizing a girl's love life involve something a little less terrifying? Something on the ground?*

"Are you sure this monster has a perfect record?" She climbed into the swinging blue car and nodded at the yellow-and-black sign that read: DANGER: KEEP YOUR HANDS AND FEET IN THE CAR AT ALL TIMES. Like anyone was going to try and bust out of this cage.

Jake climbed in behind her and tucked her in his arms. "I'm sure."

A loud clicking sound ratcheted up her fear, and the car swung out as the wheel turned, lifting them into the night sky. A small cry escaped her as they climbed higher, colored lights swirling all around them, the dark sandy beach disappearing beneath their feet.

As the wheel approached the top, Jake brushed a kiss across her temple before the car tumbled over the edge, practically swinging into the car in front of them. Her heart leaped into her throat, and yet, she still felt safe with him. The park's closing fireworks exploded all around them, and she turned to let her lips meet his, feeling brave despite her pounding heart, certain this terrifying moment, wrapped up in the arms of this nice guy, would be the most romantic moment of her life.

"I need to kiss you again," he whispered against her lips. "Not just once. All night."

"All night," she said, wrapping her elbows around his neck, entwining her fingers deep into his dark hair, and melting into his arms.

• • •

The park bustled with the happy crowd of late summer patrons, couples holding hands, kids eating funnel cake and Italian ice, teenagers making out under the colorful lights of the B&B Carousell. Jake linked his fingers through hers, and gave them a squeeze, feeling like a kid himself.

As they meandered toward the exit, he bent to give her a quick kiss, savoring the taste of her lips mixed with her mint chocolate chip ice cream. Sweet. But not as sweet as the woman. Smiling up at him, she licked the cone. Sexy, too. He smiled back at her, feeling at home in a way he hadn't for a long time. Maybe, ever.

"Game for another bit of research?"

"Does it involve more kissing?"

"Possibly."

Still smiling, she said, "Then I'm game."

With her hand in his, they criss-crossed toward the front of the park through the graffiti-laden tunnels and under the

Coney Island archway, the exit ablaze in shining red and gold lights. Passed the gate, they continued down the boardwalk. The sky was a deep shade of navy, lit by the stars, the glowing carnival lights of the park, and the arcades along the boardwalk.

"Do you like baseball?" he asked.

She gave him a sidelong glance. "Don't tell me your lesson plan involves me throwing a strikeout."

"Baseball is plenty romantic," he said, continuing before she could argue the point, "but no, you won't be tossing any pitches tonight." He smiled and looked over at the old site of Steeplechase Park, one of Brooklyn's original amusement parks, now occupied by MCU Park, a Minor league baseball stadium, home to the Brooklyn Cyclones, the Mets minor league team. When he was a kid, he'd sneak down here to listen to the games from outside the place. "Maybe I'll take you to a game sometime."

She nodded, a quizzical expression on her face as she dove back into her mint chocolate chip. "I'd like that."

Jake understood the look. But just because their relationship was meant to be short-term didn't mean he couldn't take her to a ball game when he was in the city. Or was that exactly what it meant? Next time he showed up, would she be with someone else? He gave her hand another squeeze, tucked her close against his body, and cut down the planked boardwalk toward Brighton Beach.

Tucked away near the ocean was a small playground, a slide, a few swings, the red paint chipping in places. Not much. But he'd spent a lot of afternoons here throwing a ball against the slide, looking at the park rides, breathing in the ocean air. He'd felt safe here. Safer than at home, and he wanted to share this place and this moment with her.

"Here we are," he said, gesturing toward the park.

She finished her cone, tossed her napkin into a nearby

metal trashcan, and wandered toward the play set. A smile lit up her face as she touched the silver links of the swing's chain. "I never knew this was here. This is amazing."

The edge of his mouth lifted in wry agreement, knowing the chain was beat up and bound to be worn rusted in places, and charmed by her obvious enjoyment of the place. "Not as swanky as the bigger park farther down the boardwalk. But I spent a lot of time here as a kid."

She slipped onto one of the swings. "I can see you here, sporting a pair of red-hot swimming trunks, racing your friends up from the beach."

Jake dug his hands into his pockets. "Definitely no red-hot swim trunks. Mostly, I was on my own. A bit of a loner. Not many friends." When she didn't respond, he continued. "Life as a kid was okay. Most of our neighbors supported my mom. Watched out for us, tried to make sure we stayed out of trouble, which in the case of my brother…"

"Pretty tough."

He smiled. He'd forgotten she knew Nick. "Yes, pretty tough." He stepped behind the swing and gave her a gentle push. "But good as the neighbors were…no one wanted their kids around my dad, so…"

"No friends hanging out watching baseball."

"Not unless the kid was the bookie's kid." He gave the swing another push. "I spent a lot of time on my own. Jane worked at the pizza shop, Nick was busy chasing girls, and I was here, throwing the baseball against the slide, fielding it like I was a shortstop for the Yankees."

She arched back to look at him, a smile on her face. "Sounds pretty lonely."

"Maybe." Truth was it had been bitterly lonely. "Worked out. I spent a lot of time getting real good at baseball. Earned a scholarship, studied, got a break with the book." He sat on the swing next to her.

"I'd have been your friend."

Jake smiled back at her, prettier here in the moonlight than he'd ever seen her, not the kind of girl who would've looked twice at him in his ratty tennis shoes, carrying the secondhand baseball glove his brother had bought him at Goodwill.

"Hey." She dragged her feet in the sand to bring her swing to a stop. "I definitely would have been your friend."

But with a heart as sweet as her smile, he could almost believe it. He caught the edge of her swing and tugged her close. "And I definitely would've wanted to kiss you."

She reached for the chain of his swing and inched closer. "So what are you waiting for? You did say there might be some kissing."

"I did. I said there might…possibly…be kissing," he said, brushing his lips against hers as he spoke.

"I really like kissing you," she murmured as her swing bumped into his.

He sunk his hands into her hair, tugging her closer. "Enjoying every minute. Being spontaneous and playful is an important part of a healthy love life."

"Brave. Spontaneous. Playful." Their swings now entwined, she balanced her hands on his shoulders to deepen the kiss, pulling away to gaze into his eyes. "Got it."

"And intimate."

"*Definitely* intimate."

Looking into her eyes, Jake felt awed by the fact that he was here, on this beat-up swing set in the shadow of the park's golden lights, kissing this woman. A wave crashed behind them. Just a friends-with-benefits relationship. The thought kicked him in the stomach. Maybe he hadn't worked it all through. She was a Relationship girl. But relationships were his thing, too. His expertise. Had he miscalculated? He wanted to tell her everything, but she pulled his mouth down to her in a mint-chocolate kiss that was sweeter than any he'd known. And all rational thought disappeared. They remained there in the moonlight, legs entwined, swings bumping up against one another, kissing until they were both breathless, until mere kissing simply wasn't enough.

"Ready to get out of here?" She nodded, her cheek buried, warm against his neck. "Your place or mine?" he teased.

She lifted her chin, a smile pulling at the edge of her lips. "Mine's closer."

"Your place it is."

Chapter Fourteen

Outside the park, Jake flagged down a cab, and they tumbled inside, lips locked in endless kisses, speeding through the city to her walk-up, where she was pretty sure they'd have some more guaranteed-to-be-great sex. When they spilled out of the cab onto the sidewalk in front of her building, she felt breathless and hopeful.

Hopeful.

Damn.

She couldn't afford the emotions swirling inside her. Stick to the plan. Stop chasing love. Let love find her. Unless it already had? She kissed him again, slowly, softly, not daring to give in to hope. But did she feel love in his kiss? "Coming in?"

His gaze locked onto hers, he simply nodded, and as the taxi sped away from the curb, she took his hand and drew him up the steps outside her front door. As they stumbled up the flights of stairs leading to her apartment, they stopped to kiss, his hands at her waist, his body pressing her into the quiet corners of each landing. The summer air was warm. Their breathing soft and full of longing, a contrast to the bustling sounds of the Brooklyn street.

By the time they reached the top, Kate felt dizzy—from the breathless climb or the effect of his lips on her skin, she wasn't sure. As she fumbled with the keys, he leaned in and planted his hands against the wall on either side of her, kissing her lips, drifting to her jaw, coasting down her neck. She twisted the doorknob, and together they stumbled into the apartment, the light of the full moon streaming into the window by the fire escape. With their mouths entwined, he pivoted and pressed her back against the door, closing it behind them.

As his lips moved across hers in a sweet, persuasive kiss that seemed to shift around the pieces of her heart, she let go a sigh, and when he pulled away, the loss of his kiss left her aching for another. They stood there for a moment, his fingertips against her hot cheeks, her breath shallow and soft, wanting more, wanting him. Unable to wait a second longer, she reached up and brought his lips crashing back down to hers, a move that seemed to be all the invitation he needed.

His hands found the hem of her dress, lifting it over her hips to press his palm against her hot, wet core. Another sigh escaped her parted lips as his fingers slipped beneath the lace of her panties to find her clit. She let go a quiet moan as the thrill of his caress moved through her body, setting her on fire. Her body arched toward him, practically begging for more. And he seemed more than willing to please her. His lips traveled over the vulnerable cove of her throat while his free hand moved up to cup her ass to tilt her closer to his touch while his fingers worked their magic inside her. God, he was driving her crazy, circling her, drawing her close to a climax.

"I want you now, Jake," she said, her voice filled with longing. "Tonight. Tomorrow."

"Kate…" Her name fell from his lips like a promise as he tugged the provocative lace over her thighs and calves.

"God…Kate…"

Her hips angled closer toward him, desperate for a moment of release. She bit down on her bottom lip to keep from crying out as he coaxed her body to the brink only to pull away. Her head fell back on a desperate sigh as his fingers pulled away, leaving her body trembling. On a wild groan, he grabbed her ass in his hands and lifted her against him. Her elbows locked around his broad shoulders, her legs wrapped around his hips.

"I want you, too." His mouth slammed down on her lips, kissing her as he strode across the small living space toward her bedroom. She returned his kiss, angling closer, wanting him with a desperation she'd only ever felt with this man.

Cradling her against him, he let his tongue intertwine with hers as they fell back against the bed in a hot, needy tangle. Jake pressed her back against the bed, lifted the skirt back over her reaching hips. "You are beautiful."

His palms ran along the tender curve of her thighs, inching them apart so he could caress her with his tongue. The first playful flick made her cry out. But it was only the beginning. Desire pooled low in her abdomen as he worked her over with his tongue. Her desperate body arched and bucked against him, but his hands locked her hips in place, refusing to let her move even an inch. When she thought she could take no more, he raised his lips to her right breast and took her aching nipple into his mouth, his mouth warm against her heated skin, sucking on her flesh. Her core was wet and slick, her body trembling. He murmured his encouragement, letting his thumbs graze the tips of her breasts. Her eyes drifted shut.

"Look at me," he said, his voice low and commanding.

Her gaze found his and held on as he continued to stroke and tease, her body aching with the need to feel him inside her. Unable to wait one crazy second longer, her hands tore at the button of his cargos, yanking down the zipper, tugging down the shorts and then the sexy boxer briefs with her toes to free the hard, delicious length of him.

A smile melted across her face as desperation played across his features. She took his cock in her hands, unable to fight her desire to touch him so intimately, to see his barriers fall away. She loved the feel of him in her hands, so hard and yet so vulnerable to her touch. His body trembled as her hand moved up and down his shaft, and she felt him harden further in her grasp. A deep growl rumbled up from his throat, and he reached for her hands, pinning them back against the bed with one hand while he positioned his rock-hard erection above her.

He pulled a condom from the pocket of his shorts with his free hand and tore it open with his teeth. "Don't move," he commanded. She didn't dare. She only watched as he slid the protection over his cock. She was barely breathing, her body aching and desperate to feel him inside her. "I am going to make you feel the way you've never felt before."

"Is that a guarantee?" she asked, breathless, still staring, not moving.

He held her wrists above her head with one hand while the other slowed below her hips. "That's a promise."

He bent to give her a slow, lingering kiss as his cock inched inside her. He rocked her gently, increasing the rhythm as her breath grew ragged. Small sounds of need fell from her lips as she bucked against him, her arms pinned to the bed, her legs wrapped around his waist.

"Come for me, Kate, don't hold back. I want to hear you come for me."

With both hands on her hips, he drove her harder, thrusting down as he rode her body toward climax. She threw her head back, crying out as she reached a shattering orgasm, colored waves of pleasure crashing through her.

He slowed his pace momentarily, sliding in and out of her,

drawing out her climax until she sighed with pleasure. Her hips rose up to meet the now-quickening pace of his thrusts, until his strong body tensed, before falling against her in pleasure and release.

Their bodies still locked together, he kissed her breathless. Then once again his lips drifted down the lines and curves of her body, touching her, tasting her, making good on his promise to make her feel things she'd never felt before.

Her one-night stand was officially a double score, and as her body quivered under the delights of his tongue, she held his gaze and watched him work her body with the magic of his tongue, gripping the edge of the bed as her body began to tremble.

YES.

YES.

YES.

Chapter Fifteen

Kate woke up with the weight of Jake's naked body pressed up against her back, his arm draped around her, all casually intimate and cozy. The Morning After, Take Two. Definitely better than the first, she thought, looking at his sleeping form, the sheet low on his hips. Better because he was still here, in the bed, looking delicious and cool.

"Morning." The warm sound of his voice sent an impossible thrill of pleasure down her spine. A sexy-as-sin smile touched his mouth as he rolled onto his right hip, allowing the sheet to dip a little lower. More than anything, she wanted him to stay. Her confounded romantic heart wanted to see him in the morning. Feel the naked length of him next to her. Hear that voice. See that smile. Rise up to meet him as he buried himself inside her.

"Morning." Even to her own ears, her voice echoed with longing.

Jake reached out and tucked a curl behind her ear. Dropped a kiss on her mouth. Smiled. "I have to go."

Kate blinked. Of course, he did. Yes, she'd expected

bagels and morning sex. Not in that order, but he needed to go. Panic took up residence in an open corner of her heart. What had she expected? For him to stay? Drop down on one knee? *Cuddle?*

"I'm meeting Nick to go over the contract for my next book, but dinner later?"

She nodded vaguely, knowing he was about to leave her bed, wanting him to stay.

"I thought dinner was too traditional," she said, attempting a casual humor she didn't feel.

He gave her his most wicked smile, his hands skimming the curve of her hips, dipping under the sheet to give her ass an affectionate squeeze. "Oh, we are way past traditional dates and conversation."

Despite her brain knowing better, her body grew hot, scandalously ready to give it another go. But he was already climbing out of the bed. Beautifully, perfectly naked—and leaving. *Again.*

Been here. Seen it, she thought, pulling the sheet up to her shoulders.

Jake smiled dutifully as he pulled on his jeans and yanked the T-shirt over his head, but the distance was there *again.* Physical—*check*. Emotional—*check*.

As he bent to drop a kiss onto her mouth, she reached up to frame his face in her hands lingering in a kiss that was meant to be a token, not a guarantee.

But he held her gaze sweetly. "I'll call you later."

Kate nodded, an understanding smile plastered on her face. "Don't you need a cab?"

"Nope. I'm going to take a walk over to the bridge, so I'll just catch one there."

And then, he was gone. As the door closed behind him, a sigh escaped from somewhere deep inside. She knotted the sheet between her fingers. Last night had been earth-shattering, easily the best sex of her life. Because sex with him just kept getting better. As if their bodies had been designed to work together. She'd known how to move with him, known what he needed, known exactly where to touch him to push him over the edge. Like their bodies had known each other for years. Connecting pieces of the same puzzle. Divided halves looking to come together, looking to be reunited. *Like soul mates.*

Her heart stopped. No, she shoved the sheet aside, not like soulmates. More like Three Days to Remember. That's all he'd offered. He'd promised her three days and an exclusive, and now the end of their affair was approaching. Soon it would be over — like a sexual drive-by. He'd wrap up his business, go back to his peaceful island, and she'd be back at square one. *Why did I think it would be any different?* She'd signed on for an interview — not love, not a relationship.

Rather than lie in bed, stewing over her emotions, she slid out of bed, ready to organize her ideas for her spec piece. A shower would give her perspective. A seriously cold shower, she thought, grabbing her seersucker robe.

Walking toward the bathroom, she caught a glimpse of a sheaf of folded papers peeking out from beneath the bed. Recognizing the bold red *SMART CUPID, Inc.* across the top, she picked it up and unfolded what was obviously a contract. An *unsigned* contract for her exclusive on Jake's new book — *No Strings Attached.* Her heart stuttered in her chest. *No Strings Attached?*

Kate felt a small stab of pain in her chest. *That's how I inspired him?*

She fell back onto the bed, the contract in her shaking hands. She'd convinced herself she could manage an intense attraction that went nowhere but the bedroom, but now, holding this black-and-white contract, knowing how she'd *inspired* him, it was soul crushing.

Because she was in love with him.

Dammit. She'd gone and fallen for another super-hot, super-unavailable guy. A familiar tightness started like she was going to lose her breath. All his talk about being brave and embracing the unexpected. All his sweet kisses and the amazing sex. All these hours she'd been falling in love, and he'd just been stringing her along. *Just picking up where we left off.*

He wasn't looking for a relationship. He was looking for three days while he was in town. She'd known that. Miraculously, she'd come home from the island with her heart in one piece, but here in the city—she'd fallen. Tears stung at the back of her eyes. She'd never be New Kate because she was still Old Kate, falling in love with the wrong guys. Only this time hurt a lot more.

How stupid could she be, thinking this guy who couldn't open his heart was going to come through for her? All along it was just a way to get her into bed for "research" for his book. And without a signed contract for the exclusive she wouldn't even have *Cosmo.*

She blinked back tears. What had she expected when he'd shown up all hot and gorgeous? *Swear never, ever, under any circumstances, no matter how charming he seems, no matter much he says he needs you…to fall for another super-hot guy.* Would she *never* learn?

Kate was shaking when her phone chimed into her frustration. She glanced at the screen. *Don't hyperventilate. Do. Not. Hyperventilate.* On her *Cosmo* feed, there was a breaking news banner announcing that Jake Wright's new book entitled *No Strings Attached* was due out in February. Staring at the screen, her aching, over-stuffed heart started to crack.

No—Strings—Attached.

Apparently, he'd signed *that* contract. The man left her

bed, clearly committed to his no-strings theory... Had he just been using her? Sweet, other-oriented Kate had refused to turn in the bachelor profile — *his bachelor profile* — risking her career because some intimacies were private, and yet, here he was selling their intimate encounter to all of Manhattan. She closed her eyes and tried not to let the sense of betrayal take root.

No Strings Attached. She should have known better. Hell, she had known better, she'd just been so distracted by him showing up in New York.

Kissing her. Seducing her with guaranteed great sex. Leaving her broken-hearted.

She'd believed he was different. Had she been wrong?

She needed to know.

Trading her robe for clean sweatpants, she grabbed a hoodie and dragged it across her shoulders. As she zipped the front, she shoved her feet into a pair of slip-on sneaks and picked up her keys and the contract. Minutes later, she burst out the front door of her building. She looked up and down the street, trying to imagine which direction he'd gone. *Right or left?*

Toward the bridge. She turned right and ran up the street so fast she thought the pieces of her heart might burst from her throat. Her sneakers hitting the pavement beat out a rhythm. Had she been wrong? Had she been wrong? The tree-lined street passed in a blur. Every step brought her closer to him. Closer to answers.

At Orange, she turned left toward the park, and just past the white cast-iron building on the corner of Columbia Heights and Cranberry, she saw him. Her heart leaped to her throat. She stopped in the middle of the cobblestone sidewalk. Part of her wanted to turn back, forget she'd found the contract, forget the book, forget everything except how he made her feel. How she loved him. But her sense of betrayal cut too deep. Had she been so wrong?

She drew in a breath. "Jake."

He turned immediately, the sweetest smile on his face. He waved and walked toward her. *Keep breathing. Keep breathing.*

"Hey, decide to join me? I was about to cut up to the park to grab a cup of coffee." He closed the distance between them, still smiling, until…his gaze drifted to the contract she clutched in her hand. He looked up at her, a sudden tension pulling at his features.

She held out the contract. "You left this behind."

"Kate, I can explain." He stepped toward her and she took her own step back.

"You never meant for me to have the exclusive."

Jake shook his head. "Not true—I did. I do. It's just that I'm still trying to work through the details of the book with my publisher and I didn't want—"

Kate held up a palm to stop him. She had heard enough. More than enough. "No strings attached? Is that it? Is that really all I am to you? A three day bootie call in the city?"

A muscle ticked in his jaw. "Kate, that's not fair."

Fair? Fair? What does he know about fair? "Because you are so much more me to me than some convenient, no-strings arrangement. I love you, Jake."

"Kate, please…"

"No, I do." She choked back a few tears, "Stupid, *stupid* me, dating disaster that I am, I love you."

"Listen, you can have the exclusive…"

"Jake, this is not about some exclusive, some theory or hypothetical—I love you."

He shoved his hands deep into his pockets. "Kate, I swear, let me manage the shit with the book, and when I'm done I'll answer any question you have, do anything you want."

She lifted her eyes to catch his gaze. "Anything but love

me."

He looked away. She had her answer. A new kind of pain settled in the middle of her chest. If she thought her heart was broken before…

The early morning sun shined through the trees, creating dappled shadows on the sidewalk. Obviously, she meant nothing to him. Looking at him standing on the side street in Brooklyn, more beautiful than ever, her cracked heart broke apart. Into more pieces than she could count. She wondered if a heart this shattered could ever be whole again.

"Kate, I'm sorry. I'm not built for love."

"But I am." More than anything, she'd wanted love, and he was a man who refused to believe in relationships. *What did I expect?*

"I know, and maybe that's why I'm so afraid I'll just hurt you in the long run."

"Hurt me in the long run?" *So this is my fault? Can't he see he's hurting me now?* He reached for her hand, and she wrapped her arms around her torso. If she let him touch her, she'd cry, and she was not about to let him see her cry at the thought of losing him.

He shoved his hands back into his pockets. "The fact that you are so open to love is part of what draws me to you, but I can't give you what you need. Maybe after all the shit I've been through, my heart doesn't work that way…maybe I'm just broken."

A sad smile touched her lips. "You're not broken. You're just hiding."

"Kate, God *please*, I'm sorry."

She shook her head. "Don't be."

After all, she was the one who kept telling herself it was okay, that maybe she didn't need love and all of that stuff. But her heart was fully on the line, and already in for a world of hurt, she needed to walk away right now.

"I'll have to take a rain check on that coffee." She turned to go. "Oh, and dinner, too."

"Kate."

Don't look back. Do not look back. Do. Not. Look. Back.

Kate gathered her hoodie close and continued walking, away from the park. She'd needed answers. Now, she had them. He was a man who refused to believe in relationships. Always would be. And for better or worse, after her heart healed—if her heart managed to heal—she'd still be the girl looking expectedly for love.

· · ·

An hour later, Jake stood outside the bar in Tribeca, a dull pain centered in his chest. What had the woman expected? After all the times he'd revealed himself, his feelings about privacy, how celebrity had torn his marriage apart, his life. He thought she understood. Thought she was different. His jaw tightened. He never should have come back home.

And writing another book? What had made him think this time around would be any different? *Because of her?* Yes, he'd called it *No Strings Attached*. It was just a theory, for Christ's sake. He never promised her anything. Anything more than great sex, anyway.

He'd always known he'd never be able to give her the fantasy...the love that lasts forever. Because more than guarantees and amazing sex and romantic nights at Coney Island, than her real, true fantasy. *Love*. The one thing he couldn't give. He'd come to the city, thinking...*maybe*.

He *was* broken, and yet, somewhere inside him, he'd thought...maybe...and now she'd gone and broken him all over again. Given up on him. Walked away. *Fine*. He'd refocus. Wrap up his business. Go back to the island.

Hell, he simply hadn't wanted to fail her in the end. And

what had she said? *You're not broken. You're hiding.* Well, so be it.

He shoved aside any remaining doubts and walked into the bar. The last time he'd seen his friend Charlie's bar, Temptation had been a small neighborhood joint. But this morning, with the race for the pennant on television and Bloody Marys flowing, the place bustled with a crowd of regulars, probably thanks to the publicity from the jaw-dropping bet his sister had made last year. On one of the morning shows. Always the matchmaker, she'd bet she could match any man in the city. Took a while, but she won, and now Jane and Charlie's engagement was practically an urban legend.

At a table near the back of the bar, Nick, his older brother, was already going over the details of his contract. Formerly described as a bad boy, Nick was a partner at his law firm now, a position he'd damned well earned, and newly-married to the sweet girl from Jane's office, the one who'd jumped out of his birthday cake. A bespectacled computer whiz wasn't his brother's usual type, but she'd jumped out of a cake. *Yeah, exactly his type.*

Jake walked over to the table, clapped his brother on the shoulder, and sat down. Nick pulled his Yankees cap low on his brow and set the contract on the hardwood table. His long legs stretched under the table, and he crossed his arms over his chest and nodded at the paper. "Sign it. Give him the book and you'll be legally free of the asshole who banged your wife."

"Correction," Jake said, comforted by his brother's direct approach. "Ex-wife."

Nick nodded. "Ex-wife."

Charlie came back from the bar and set a round of Bloody Marys down on the table. "Isn't she now the asshole's wife?"

Jake made a mocking sound in the back of his throat and

lifted his drink in a toast, feeling like no time had passed. "To freedom."

Nick and Charlie tilted their drinks, the glasses all meeting in the middle. Three childhood friends from Brooklyn.

His brother sipped at his drink. "To freedom."

"To freedom." Charlie sat down at the table.

Jake took a long sip of the spicy vodka drink. "Except you two aren't exactly free."

Both guys focused their attention on the Mets game playing on the television behind the bar, neither ready to cop to being beaten by love. Jake tilted his glass toward his brother. "I mean, you're married." He turned toward Charlie with a smile on his face. "And buddy, you are definitely on the ropes."

Charlie waved him off. "I'm not on the ropes."

Nick nodded in agreement. "Yeah, he's not on the ropes. He's done. Finished. The whole situation with our sister was embarrassing, really."

"Lovestruck?" Jake teased, his voice full of mock-pity.

Nick leaned toward his brother. "After they broke up the first time, the man spent months talking about emotional honesty."

Charlie grinned. "Emotional honesty—isn't that your area of expertise, Jake? You're the sexpert in the group."

Jake chuckled and shook his head. "Ex-sexpert to you, buddy, and don't think you're getting out of this one. When are you going to make our sister an *emotionally honest* woman?"

"God, please," Nick said, tugging at his dark hair, "I can't take many more conversations about the wedding."

Charlie rolled his eyes. "You are *not* the only one." He jumped to his feet, waving his Mets cap at the television. "Did you see that hit? Did you—that's it, that's the ballgame." He sat back down and grinned at Nick. "Next time we play pool, you're buying, buddy."

"Will you stop betting on the Yankees, bro. Every time you lay down money, they lose."

Nick threw a twenty onto the table. "Just a friendly side wager."

"So, what about you and love, Jake?" Catching the young bartender's eye, Charlie gestured for him to flip to ESPN before turning back to the table. "Who brought you out of hiding?"

Nick choked back some of his drink but failed to hide his amusement. "He means, back to Manhattan."

He offered a casual shrug. "The book, the apartment."

Charlie looked at Nick. "I heard it was a woman."

"Not a woman." *Not as of this morning, that's for damn sure.* Jake knew these guys were looking for a reaction, but he just swirled the Bloody Mary around in his glass, ice cubes clinking against the sides, aiming for cool. "Yes, there was a woman, but it was a no-strings situation." He cocked an eyebrow. "No offense to you two, but commitment's overrated." Although the truth was his "new gold standard of relationships" was starting to feel a tad hollow.

Nick leaned way back in his chair. "Right—overrated."

"I'm not interested in marriage."

Charlie ran a hand over his five-o'clock shadow. "God knows the first one was a disaster."

"A complete disaster," Nick agreed.

"Total devastation."

"Hurricane Sally."

"Worse than a hurricane," Jake confirmed, thinking his last experience with a hurricane was pretty damned fantastic. "A *tornado*."

They stared at the middle of the table, silent.

"Women," Charlie said.

"Can't live with 'em," Nick started the familiar adage.

"Can't love without 'em," Charlie finished, and his friends

raised their glasses in silent tribute. "Course it is a little strange, a sex therapist being so bad with women."

"I'm not bad with women," Jake said on a defensive sigh. "Not all women, anyway. This woman...she was *different*." He set the drink down and rotated the glass on the table. "Beautiful and sweet and funny. Amazing with a power tool. Totally down with the food at Spicy Village. But she had this crazy thing about airplanes and Ferris wheels."

Nick offered up a casual nod. "So you took her to Coney Island?"

He took another sip from his drink to cover the fact that he'd sounded more like a guy in love than a guy letting go of a no-strings situation. So much was riding on his new theory, getting this book out into the marketplace. Honestly, Kate had done him a favor this morning. He needed to move on, and the book was his ticket. "Yes, I took her to Coney Island."

All casual and cool, Nick asked, "When was the last time you were there?"

Jake eyed his brother with suspicion. "You know when."

His brother flashed one of his brash, you-can't-hide-from-me grins, the kind that had always made him confess when they were kids. "Didn't you swear you'd never go back?"

"Jesus, what is this, counselor?" Jake asked, trying for humor but missing the mark by a mile. "A cross-examination?"

"Kiss her at the top?" he asked in full-on lawyer mode, already drawing his conclusion. "Yeah, you definitely kissed her at the top."

Jake rolled his eyes and moved his glass in a circle on the table.

Charlie took a sip of his drink. Nick gave an easy shrug of his shoulder. "Not on the ropes."

Charlie grinned. "Nope."

Jake gave a short nod. "Thank you—at least somebody here knows the deal."

"Yeah, he's already down for the eight-count." Charlie raised his glass in the air to meet Nick's with a definite clink.

. . .

An hour later, Jake left the bar, having endured enough ribbing and bad sports metaphors to last a lifetime. Head bent toward the cobblestone and crossed over Chambers Street, the morning sun shining, the blue neon light of the bar's signage reflecting his thoughts. Temptation. A small smile touched his lips. Kate was definitely that, and if he was honest, so much more.

He'd take her to dinner tonight and broach the subject of seeing her again. If all went well, there'd be a book tour. Trips to the city. Enough to work something out. Not exactly no-strings, not a commitment, but…hell, he didn't know. Sure, he'd written another book, but he was still no expert. Spotting the famous green-and-gold hot dog cart on the other side of the street, he crossed against the light. Couldn't get Nathan's in Paradise. Best to get it now. But before he could get there, his phone buzzed in his pocket.

After digging it out, he swiped over to look at the message. A tweet appeared on the screen, something his ex-agent must've set up — although he never mentioned a media blitz. Typical of the asshole to move ahead without consulting him. He tapped on the screen and the Tweet appeared.

@Cosmopolitan Jake Wright's long-awaited new book entitled No Strings Attached out this February. #havemoresex #loveit

Jake stopped in the middle of the street and had to move to avoid being clipped by a taxi. *What the hell?* Why was *Cosmo* tweeting about his book?

He swiped again and a list of social media hits splashed

onto the screen. His cell chimed, so he flipped to messages and found several texts full of drink requests and potential dinner dates. A few dating profiles in the list even included photos. *Jesus.* He started to sweat. Already back to that counterfeit celebrity-style life where everybody wanted a piece of him. Shit, the book wasn't even finished, and he was being assaulted by a media blitz and date requests from women on his iPhone.

Jesus, *No Strings Attached* was a *working* title. Yes, it was basically finished, but it was still a work in *progress* and, honestly, since dropping back into Manhattan, being with Kate, making love to her…here…back home…he'd started thinking…the hell with what he'd been thinking. All that was over now. Water under the Brooklyn Bridge.

Or was it? Had she sent in the profile after their breakup this morning? If you called ending a no-strings situation a *breakup*? Had she played him by sending in the bachelor profile? So she could follow it up with an exclusive on his new book? Selling him out as some win-a-date bachelor, betraying every minute they'd spent together, every intimacy they shared. No. That was bonkers. That wasn't Kate. Yes, she'd been hurt and angry. Hell, he was furious with himself for his mistake, but that didn't mean she'd done anything on his level. He was the asshole. Not her. But still, the whole thing didn't add up.

He turned on his heels and strode back down to Chambers to catch a cab over to the Smart Cupid office where he hoped to find her—and some answers.

• • •

Fifteen long minutes later, Jake strode into his sister's office. "What the hell?"

Jane looked up from her desk, cool as a damned fruit smoothie, as if she'd been expecting him. "I know, it's unexpected, but the publicity might be a good thing."

"Jane, you know how I feel about all the celebrity bullshit."

"Jake, you wrote the book. Did you expect no one would read it?" She gave him a look that said *be serious*. "Did you think you'd roll back into Manhattan without anyone noticing? *Come on.*"

He tore both hands through his hair. Took a breath. Tried to stay calm. "Where's *Kate*?"

"Not that it's any of your business, but she's working from home today, and FYI, *Kate* had nothing to do with…*the situation.*"

"The situation. You mean my surprise publicity blitz?" he said, his voice laced with irritation.

Jane paused, opened her candy drawer and took out a Twix, a Snickers, and a King-sized pack of Twizzlers.

Jake took in the sugar-laden stash. *Shit, this is a three-candy-bar problem. What the hell is she going to say next?*

"So, you haven't seen the *Cosmo* article?" Jane asked.

Dread seeping through his system, Jake dug his phone from his pocket. "What *Cosmo* article?"

He swiped his screen and dozens of new tweets stared back at him.

@Cosmopolitan Hey, Cosmo girls, check out Jake Wright's bachelor profile on our website today. #nostringsattached.

@Cosmopolitan Is Jake your Mr. Wright. Enter now to win a date with Manhattan's favorite sexpert #nostringsattached

@Cosmopolitan Sexpert Jake Wright talks boxers, blondes & fantasy. Bachelor Profile on newsstands next week. #nostringsattached

"Oh my God."

A tight smile stretched across his sister's face. "You're trending."

"This is a nightmare." He swiped a hand across his face. "How the hell... So this wasn't that son-of-a-bitch ex-agent... she turned in the damned bachelor interview."

"No, *she* didn't." Jane drew in a breath and confessed on the exhale. "Kate didn't turn in the profile. *I did.*"

He reached down deep and tried to stay calm. "Janey, I told you, *no way in hell.* I don't want to be an Internet bachelor." He flipped the phone around so she could see it. "*Win a Date With Mr. Wright.* Seriously?"

"I never meant for the magazine to *publish* it," Jane said, apology in her tone. "I only sent it over to get Kate a shot at *Cosmo.* Hell, she earned it—flying off to that damn island of yours, dealing with your issues, cracking open that walled up heart of yours."

Jake collapsed onto the loveseat and stared at the screen. "Jesus, I don't want to be a *bachelor.* I want..." He let his words trail off.

Jane sighed. "I leaked the information about the new book, too. The exclusive interview was going to be Kate's big shot at her dream job."

He looked at Jane. "What do you mean *cracking open that heart of yours?*"

"Does it matter?" His sister raised an eyebrow. "Thought you wanted no strings."

No strings? But did that mean he had to be alone forever?

"Hold on," he said. "Was this whole thing a setup?"

"I thought something *might* happen between you two."

A smile lifted the edges of his mouth. "You got good aim, Cupid."

Jane looked at him, smiling back. "*Damn good.*"

Chapter Sixteen

Maybe she should move back to Ohio. She'd spent the last few days trying to piece her heart back together. She'd even gone back to Coney Island to ride The Wheel, knowing it was time to conquer her own fears. To be brave, not for a relationship, for *herself*.

She'd walked all over the city. Spent days crossing items off her New York bucket list. Practiced Tai Chi in Columbus Park. Went to the boathouse in Central Park. Indulged at Serendipity.

But nothing stopped the ache in her heart.

More than three days had passed, so Jake was obviously back on the island, enjoying his peace, and she was still here, sitting on the apartment-sized sofa in her walk-up. *Why not move back to Ohio?* She'd written up a spec piece, not the exclusive, but a piece called "Making Over Your Love Life." She'd emailed it directly to the editor at *Cosmo*, but she'd heard nothing. Even after Jane's recommendation. *No exclusive. No* Cosmo.

Maybe she really was just the blonde girl from Ohio,

destined to marry the neighbor's son and wear a hard hat for the rest of her life. *Don't hyperventilate. Do. Not. Hyperventilate.* No—she just needed to think.

Obviously, she needed to stop dating. Completely. Even her walk on the wild side had turned out to be a disaster. Was this really what she inspired? Men taking off? Leaving donuts? No strings? No love? Because her relationship with Jake had felt different—*real*. She eyed her cell phone. Not wanting more news of her so-called bachelor, she'd turned the damn thing off hours ago, but now she wondered if she ought to call him. Give him a chance to explain. No—she didn't need an explanation. She had needed her exclusive. Even if he hadn't signed the contract, the man had owed her an exclusive. They'd had a verbal agreement. Although she missed all their non-verbal stuff, too. Hell, she missed him. But love had found her once, and even though he wasn't The One, despite the pain, she was happy to have experienced the kind of love she'd always believed in.

Maybe that love would find her again.

Then, just as she was about to give in and indulge in a marathon session of Dr. Phil On Demand, she heard a car horn blare outside. She wrinkled her nose. Probably a taxi. Or moving van. *Welcome to Brooklyn,* she thought. *I'll be booking a U-Haul next week.* She picked up the remote and settled in the corner of the loveseat. And that's when she heard it—the grating sound of her fire escape being pulled down. Her mind raced ahead. Someone was climbing up the fire escape. Like any good New Yorker, she carried pepper spray, but like any good Ohio girl, she'd left it in her purse. In her purse—in the closet—with her cell phone. She reached under the loveseat and picked up the baseball bat her dad had given her when she'd left for New York. Heart in her throat, she walked over to the window.

Outside, a cab was parked haphazardly on the concrete

sidewalk, and near the bottom of the twisty metal ladder stood Jake Wright, balancing a box of Krispy Kremes in his hand.

What in the world... She could have smashed him with a baseball bat. She set down the bat and opened the window, her heart racing. "What the hell are you doing here?"

Jake smiled and continued up the shaky metal to the small landing outside her window. He handed her the donuts and anchored his arm against the metal grate, looking adorably, painfully sweet in his worn denim and Yankees T-shirt. She shook her head as tears pricked at the backs of her eyes. He looked so perfect, so frustratingly, wonderfully perfect. *Dammit.* A little hope sparked in her heart all over again.

He reached for her hand. "Is that any way to talk to your soul mate?"

Her voice was quiet. "My soul mate?"

"God, I hope so." He climbed in the window in such an endearing way that she almost forgave him everything, right then and there. He took the donuts from her trembling fingers and set them on the windowsill. "Kate, I know I probably don't deserve you, but I love you. I do. I think I've loved you from the moment you tumbled down those stairs. I love that you can't handle more than one martini or a ride on the Wonder Wheel, and I'm not sure how our relationship turned into love, but it did. At least for me, and I know that I don't have to hide anymore, because this time around love is right. Maybe it's hard to believe in The One until she's standing right in front of you." He brushed a sweet kiss across her lips. "You are The One. *My* One."

There it was. Everything she wanted to hear. Everything she wanted to believe. She slipped her hands from his and bit down hard on her bottom lip. "How do you know—how do you know I'm The One?"

Jake took her hands back into in his. "Do you know what

I've been doing the past two days?"

Heart racing, she looked up at him. Unable to breathe, she shook her head.

He smiled. "I sat down, and I started rewriting the book."

The tears she'd been holding back fell down her cheeks. "Really?"

"Really." Jake framed her face in his hands. "You are the woman who empowered me to write again, to trust my instincts. The book title is all wrong. Kate, I want the strings… all the attachments. Love, family, the city—*everything*." His expression was so sweet, so earnest and true, she couldn't help but keep falling for this man all over again.

Jake wiped the tears away from her cheeks. "And do you know what I did right before I called Manhattan Taxi to drive me over here to Brooklyn?" He pressed a hard kiss on her mouth." I spent the entire morning tearing up the new floors in my apartment."

"What?" She blinked. Not sure what she'd been expecting, but ripping up perfectly good hardwood had not been on any list of possibilities. "But, that's…that's crazy."

A deep laugh exploded from his chest. He kissed her again. "I know. It is. Totally crazy, but I'm not going to sell the place. Not now, not ever, and I want to fix the floors. I want to fix *everything*…with you…only you." He smiled. She smiled right back, finally able to breathe. "You are my happiness, my fantasy, my paradise. You are my One. Let me be yours and I'll spend the rest of my life making you a believer."

"Okay."

He pressed another fast kiss on her mouth. "Okay?"

Wiping away the tears, she nodded. "Okay."

Then, as laughter bubbled up from her chest, Jake hauled her out the open window and onto the fire escape, but she knew she'd never want to escape this man. Holding her hand in his, he leaned over the edge and called out to the waiting cabbie, "She said okay!"

Then he turned back to her and pressed her back against the narrow brick wall. "I am so going to kiss you right now." And as he gathered her close and kissed her with all the passion a girl could ask for, the sound of the cabbie honking as he tore away from the curb, Kate knew she'd found her One. With the summer sun shining in the New York sky, Jake Wright gave her a sweet, mesmerizing, forever kind of kiss that seemed to shift the ground beneath her feet. Right there. On her fire escape. For all the world to see.

"I love you, Jake."

"I love you, too."

And then this man—this endearing, sexy, incredibly hot man—offered up exactly what she'd been waiting for—*hoping* for—a gaze full of promises and a kiss guaranteed to lead to some really hot chips.

Epilogue

Sunlight reflected against the turquoise water as *Island Time* drifted along the edge of the cove. The island in November was calm and peaceful, hurricane season on the horizon, but no storms in sight, a thousand miles away from the city they both loved.

Kate smiled at Jake, taking in the sight of her very own sexpert, the gorgeous man who aligned her ch'i, seduced her with sweet kisses and hot chips, and showed her that sexy is more than skin deep. *Sexy* is a state of mind.

Maybe this really *was* what Deepak Chopra meant by the Law of Least Effort. She'd stopped searching for that perfect man, stopped expending all her effort on creating the *right* kind of romantic relationship, and found The One. Or rather, he'd found her.

Her super-sized heart wasn't big enough for all the love she felt, and yet she knew her feelings would grow with every day she spent with him. By focusing on one dream, she'd made all her dreams come true, and she hadn't hyperventilated in *weeks*. Not even when the issue of *Cosmopolitan* with her first byline hit the newsstand.

After the bachelor profile fiasco, her *Cosmo* editor had apologized for leaking the story, and they'd hashed out a fair contract. Revamping her love life had brought more than a career boost or guaranteed great sex; it had brought her love—real love—and if her article brought the next girl half as much joy, Kate would finally feel like a success. As for now, well, she was pretty happy personally researching her scoop, *Making Your Love Life Go the Distance.*

Next to her, the man of her dreams gave her a sexy smile hot enough to melt her insides and pressed a rectangular package wrapped in plain brown paper into her hands. "For you."

A soft breeze warmed her skin, and she unwrapped the package to find a galley copy of Jake's second book: *Living Happily Ever After…*

His voice grew quiet. "Go ahead. Open it."

Fingers trembling, she turned to the dedication page as he spoke the words printed on the page. "*For Kate, one more question… Will you marry me?*"

Her breath caught in her throat, and the world slowed all around them. Her heart ached with the joy of his question, with the sense of hope, and of possibility that anything can happen.

Even love. Especially love.

Tears pricked at the backs of her eyes as she took in the sight of him on bended knee, a ring in his hand. Her romantic fantasy come true. "Marry me."

"Yes," she said with a watery smile. "I can't wait to marry you." She knelt next to him as the boat rocked back and forth in the waves, the world drifting by in a soft, romantic blur. "I always knew you were The One."

Jake slipped the ring on her finger. "Not exactly how I remember it."

Kate smiled. "Even when my mind believed it wasn't going to last, my heart knew you were my soul mate," she said, wrapping her arms around his neck. "Now if we could only get Jane and Charlie to tie the knot."

"Funny you should say that," he said, pulling his phone from the pocket of his shorts, "Look what showed up on my email feed this morning." Jake flipped his phone around so that she could see the words scrolling on the screen. *Looks like a certain Manhattan Cupid's tying the knot and you're invited. #cupidwedding. #brooklyn #savethedate.*

"Should we make it a double wedding?"

"Sweetheart, I plan on leaving this island a married man."

"Really?"

"Hell, yes, I intend to marry you in Paradise," he said, gathering her close in his arms, "and never let you go."

"Promise?"

"Promise." A slow, sexy smile creased his handsome face, and he moved his mouth against her ear. "Know my ultimate secret fantasy?"

She peeked over at him, her voice a hopeful whisper. "Sex on a boat?"

"Sex." His smile widened, and a wicked gleam lit up the Caribbean blue eyes she'd literally fallen head-over-heels for. "On a boat."

Acknowledgments

Writing is an adventure, a sometimes herculean task, not meant to be undertaken alone, and I'm lucky to have many people who support me through life's wonderful, challenging times.

And so, my endless thanks to Elley Arden, my friend and generous reader whose unique story ideas inspire me. To my fellow Entangled Authors and writing besties, Robin Bielman and Samanthe Beck, I can only say how crazy-lucky I am to have you as friends. One of these days Shirley Jump is going to get a big, sloppy kiss for offering the class that brought Sam Beck into my life, and introduced me to Robin Bielman. Sometime soon, we'll all be drinking wine (plenty of it) and celebrating our adventures together.

To Melissa Smith-Beckner, my BFF of almost forty years, thank you for all the madness, for encouraging me when I think—nope—and for always being there. I can't remember a time when we weren't friends.

To all the folks at Entangled. How lucky am I? To Liz Pelletier and Heather Howland, thank you for your patience and generosity and love of romance. I am so happy to be part of Entangled. Big thanks to Christine Chhun, Bridget O'Toole, and my wonderful, eagle-eyed copy editor for bringing this book across the finish line and out into the world. To Heather and Stephen Morgan for making *One Little Kiss* the absolute best it could be, and to the amazing and kiss-worthy, Vanessa Mitchell, my fab editor and an awesome chick. Your faith in me made Smart Cupid possible. What more can I say? I thank my lucky stars for you.

And to everyone who has read the Smart Cupid series, I am grateful beyond measure to each and every reader who has spent time with the series and its characters. I feel so lucky to be allowed to share these stories with you and I can't wait for what comes next.

Lastly, thank you to my husband and two little boys for managing dinner and soccer practice and baseball games and viola rehearsals. For missing me when I can't be there. For loving when I am. There's nothing and no one I love more in the world.

About the Author

After ten years of survival, aka working, in Hollywood, this former actress and current author of sexy contemporary romance is living happily-ever-after in Pittsburgh with her longtime sweetie, AKA Husband Number 1, and their two punky kids. When not carpooling to birthday parties or testing her gourmet cooking skills by throwing a frozen pizza into the oven, Maggie daydreams about sneaking off to Vegas or Napa, or even just the movies. A love of red wine, Italian food, and music round out her list of life's greatest joys. Oh, and Tuesday night karaoke, totally underrated fun.

Discover the **Smart Cupid** *series…*

BREAKING THE BACHELOR

UNEXPECTEDLY HIS

Find love in unexpected places with these satisfying
Lovestruck reads...

BETTING THE BAD BOY
a *Behind the Bar* novel by Stefanie London

Paige Thomas needs to find a job—any job—to make ends meet. Noah Reid is looking after his best friend's bar for one month, and he can't do it alone. Things get steamy when Noah hires Paige, but she bets him that she can keep her hands to herself while they work together. Too bad for her, Noah is an expert at breaking the rules...

THE 48-HOUR HOOKUP
a *Chase Brothers* novel by Sarah Ballance

With three disastrous relationships under her belt, it's clear Claire Stevens's judgment sucks. And what's she's feeling for America's newest sex god? Obviously another hormone-fueled mistake. But when a winter storm leaves them stranded in her decrepit chalet with a chocolate-snatching raccoon, there's something to be said for body heat. Falling for him wasn't the plan. But neither was their explosive chemistry...or the temptation to follow her heart one more time.

Blame it on the Kiss
a *Kisses in the Sand* novel by Robin Bielman

When Honor Mitchell promises to do the things on her dying best friend's wish list, she's determined to follow through. Then she's thrown together for wedding duties with the one man who complicates her vow—just by looking at him. Bryce Bishop's trust in women is shot, but he can't help but help Honor tick off the items on his ex's list, even if it puts him in a no-win situation. He'll help Honor get what she wants…even if being the do-good guy puts his plans—and heart—in jeopardy.

Best Man for Hire
a *Front and Center* novel by Tawna Fenske

Anna Keebler makes a living being unconventional. As a wedding planner, she specializes in more…*unusual* ceremonies. So when her photographer quits during a wedding blitz in Hawaii, Anna makes an unconventional decision. She hires a hot Marine to be her new photographer. But Anna suspects Grant Patton's sexy Boy Scout routine is a cover, and if he wants this thing between them to be more than sex, he must reveal the dark past he's fought to keep hidden.

Made in United States
Cleveland, OH
08 May 2025

16773965R00121